THE PROMISE

THE
PROMISE

Sally Jenkins

The Book Guild Ltd

First published in Great Britain in 2018 by
The Book Guild Ltd
9 Priory Business Park
Wistow Road, Kibworth
Leicestershire, LE8 0RX
Freephone: 0800 999 2982
www.bookguild.co.uk
Email: info@bookguild.co.uk
Twitter: @bookguild

Typeset in Minion Pro

Printed and bound in Great Britain by CPI Group (UK) Ltd, Croydon, CR0 4YY

ISBN 978 1912083 985

British Library Cataloguing in Publication Data.
A catalogue record for this book is available from the British Library.

For all those who have helped along the way –
your support continues to be invaluable.

1

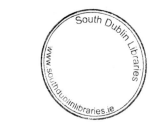

His blood went everywhere. It was warm and sticky. Olivia wiped her hands down her T-shirt and rubbed them on her jeans. She raised her palms and stared at the smeared crimson swirls. Then she looked down at the body, prone on the floor of the hallway, the wet, scarlet puddle on the front of his white T-shirt slowly expanding.

At first Olivia didn't notice the screaming but it must have been there all the time. She looked up. A middle-aged woman was staring at the corpse. Her mouth was open and she was emitting a high-pitched noise, like an animal ensnared in a trap. The woman knelt and wrapped her hands around the knife handle, as though to pull it from the man's chest.

"No! You'll make it worse!" The young male voice made Olivia jump. It was familiar but unidentifiable, the shout distorted and strangled by panic. She watched as he pulled the woman away from the body.

Then, with his back towards Olivia, the youth used an old-fashioned phone to call an ambulance. Everything she could see was old-fashioned. The gaudy orange and brown swirls on the carpet were 1970s retro. The clothes came from early in the decade that followed. The man on the floor wore a purple tracksuit with the top unzipped. The middle-aged woman had a tight curly perm and a fussy blouse with a bow tied at the neck.

The cream, curled telephone cord turned pink as the faceless male caller wrapped it around and around his fingers. He gave the emergency services the address and a single fact – a man had been stabbed. The wail of sirens was almost immediate. The noise swirled around and around in Olivia's head.

***

Blue lights beneath her eyelids and the noise of emergency vehicles dragged Olivia from the depths of sleep. It took a second to realise she wasn't still crouched in the corner of a 1980s hallway watching the aftermath of murder. She was in her own bed. She was in *their* bed. With this blessed relief came the gradual slowing of her heartbeat. Mark was making little breathing sounds. A splinter of light from a streetlamp had found the tiny gap between the curtains and highlighted the collection of freckles across the bridge of his nose. The summer sunshine of the last few weeks had darkened them and given the rest of his face a healthy glow. She wanted to hug this man. She wanted to hold him tight and never let him go. But instead of waking him, she placed a gentle, silent kiss on his cheek. Mark made her feel good about herself and, whatever the circumstances, he always believed in her. She thought about their coming wedding and a surge of joy made her grin into the darkness.

She wriggled very slowly to the edge of the bed so she could see the alarm clock. 3:15 am. Mark stirred slightly, murmured something indecipherable and turned over. Olivia put her head back on the pillow, closed her eyes and drifted towards sleep. Then she fought in vain against the pull of the swirly orange carpet. It dragged her back to the depths of terror.

"Olivia! It's OK, I've got you. You can stop screaming." Mark had his arms clamped around her.

Every muscle felt tense and ready to flee the image burning on the inside of her eyelids. The image of a dead man in a purple tracksuit, his chest perforated by a knife and leaking blood. She clenched her fists with the immense effort it took to open her eyes and banish the vision. The grunt that escaped her was involuntary.

"Hey." Mark stroked her cheek. "That little pig noise sounded like John McEnroe serving at Wimbledon."

Olivia managed a weak smile into the darkness. The duvet was skew-whiff and her pillow was disappearing down the gap between the bed and the wall.

"Bad dream?"

"Mmmm." Her voice felt thick with sleep. "What time is it?"

"Three-thirty."

How could it be only fifteen minutes since she'd checked the clock? She wormed herself away from Mark. Her palms were clammy. Slowly she held her hands out in front of her. Her heart pounded. The damp on her skin felt like the sticky blood in her dreams. That bloodied hallway had seemed so real. She stared at her hands. Were they red? The gloom of the bedroom wasn't enough to see properly.

"I need the toilet." Olivia kicked the edge of the duvet away and struggled out of bed without using her hands. She didn't want to leave a trail of bloody handprints.

She shivered in the chill of the bathroom. The cotton nightdress stuck to her body with the swiftly cooling sweat of night fear. The bathroom blind was pulled only half-way down but there still wasn't sufficient light to be sure the darkness on her hands was only shadow. She took the pull cord of the light gingerly between her thumb and forefinger. Light exploded above her. She blinked rapidly. For a second she saw herself outside a court building with a blanket over her head, getting into a police van surrounded by the exploding flashbulbs of photographers. Then she looked at her hands. Her knees buckled and she sank onto the toilet seat. Her hands were clean. No blood. She turned them over. The diamond on her left hand sparkled.

"Are you OK?" The bathroom door wasn't shut but still Mark gave a little knock.

"Fine. I'll be one minute." She heard him pad back to bed. She took the toothbrushes out of their glass, filled it with water and took a drink. In a few minutes she'd feel calm enough to go back to bed.

Mark fell asleep again quickly. Olivia was too scared to close her eyes. Twice in one night – she'd never had the nightmare twice in one night before.

***

When the cough first started Tina had ignored it. Most things got better by themselves. But this didn't. It kept her awake at night and often, by morning, her ribs and chest ached from the spasms. Wayne never said anything but she saw the look of fear in his eyes when another coughing fit wracked her body or she struggled for breath on the stairs when the lift was broken. He bought her bottles of cough medicine but they made no difference. He made her cups of tea with, what his compulsive rituals deemed, precisely the right amount of milk. Once he even brought her flowers – with a handwritten 'In Memoriam' card still attached. Tina tore up the small piece of cardboard covered in black ballpoint lettering. It was the thought that counted and Wayne had thought about her. Despite his problems with everyday life, she hadn't done too badly in the care of her brother. His heart was in the right place where family was concerned.

But Tina was scared. This was how the cancer had started with their mother and she'd been a similar age. It hadn't taken long for their mum to become terminal. Fear of the same fate eventually forced Tina to see a doctor. A stream of hospital appointments and tests followed. She managed to hide most of them from Wayne and play down the seriousness of the others. She didn't want him to know the worst until it was definite and necessary. A few minutes from now, she'd know if there was something to tell her younger brother.

Everyone else in the waiting area had someone with them. Somebody to hold their hand, mop their tears, drive them home and put the kettle on. Or, maybe, that someone would share their joy when everything proved to be negative and all the worries unfounded. Whatever the news, Tina would cope alone. She'd nod at the doctor, grit her teeth and get the bus home. Wayne would be in when she got there. He refused to go out at teatime because the TV quiz show, *Pointless,* was built into the rituals of his life. He was addicted to the programme and the contestants' battle to outwit the audience. Once, she'd insisted he help her with the supermarket shopping, they'd missed the bus home and he'd gone into meltdown as they waited for the next one. He was trembling and crying and a passer-by had had to help Tina get him onto the bus. He'd spent the journey with white knuckles gripping the seat in front. After that, they'd always gone to the supermarket in the morning. Wayne was fifty, ten years younger than Tina, but his rituals and emotional dependence on routine made it feel as though she had a five-year-old to look after.

"Tina Mallinson?" A nurse had appeared in the waiting area holding a clipboard.

Tina stood up, trying to ignore the pain in her back, and followed the nurse into the consultant's office. It was true what they said about policemen and doctors getting younger; the man in front of her looked about fifteen years old. This amazingly young consultant ran through a quick explanation of the tests they'd done and the results, all the time looking more at his computer screen than at her. Most of it went over her head. Tina needed a black and white answer. She interrupted his flow of percentage chances and survival rates.

"Doc, am I going to die of cancer? I don't want to know all these numbers. I have someone depending on me and if I'm going to die I need to make arrangements."

"But it's not as cut and dried—"

"Doctor, am I going to die? Don't hide behind your clever numbers in the hope of making me feel better. I feel lousy. And I know it's bad." She coughed and the noise echoed around the hard, clinical room. There was no carpet to absorb the sound. "Just tell me in one word. Yes or no?"

"Yes." The word was barely audible and his glance at her, before he turned back to the computer screen, hardly noticeable. He seemed unable to look her in the eye with his bad news. "But in a few patients life is prolonged by…"

Tina didn't hear the rest of what the doctor said. She focussed on the solid fact she'd been given: she was going to die in the same way her mother had. Wayne would be left alone, with no hope of holding down a job and with no one to look after him. Tina hadn't kept her promise.

Eventually the doctor's voice fell silent and Tina realised the appointment was at an end. He handed her a wodge of leaflets, which she'd never read, and a list of follow-up clinic visits. Then he shook her other hand and opened the door. In the hospital corridor she couldn't remember which way was out. For a minute she wandered up and down, confused by doorways and waiting areas that all looked the same. An elderly gentleman with a walking stick and a badge shouting 'VOLUNTEER' rescued her and accompanied her, as fast as his stick would allow, all the way to the bus stop. His monologue about the weather and the state of the city's buses lasted the whole way.

"Thanks," she said when they reached the plastic and metal shelter, which had been rendered rainbow coloured by graffiti.

The old man raised his walking-stick-free hand to his forehead in a salute. "My pleasure, madam." Then he turned and hobbled back towards the hospital complex.

When Tina got back to the flats the lift wasn't working again and she had to stop on each grimy landing to lean against the wall and rest her lungs.

"Alright, Tina?"

"How are you, Tina? How's your Wayne doing?"

She merely nodded at her neighbours who were descending as she climbed. There wasn't the breath to talk and she was anxious to get home, hide away and lick her wounds. And she had to break the news to Wayne.

The theme tune for *Pointless* was fading as she put the key in the lock. Wayne was bouncing round the flat on a high and, as soon as she walked into the lounge, he started reeling off the questions he'd scored well on.

"That's good," she spoke automatically, dropping her bag containing the hospital leaflets and sinking into the scuffed blue leather armchair. "Put the kettle on, will you?"

Making tea was the only one of Wayne's chronic rituals that was of any use to man or beast. He warmed cups, measured out loose tea into a teapot and was precise about the amount of milk. The milk had to go in first followed by the tea, which went through a strainer. Where he'd learnt all this, Tina had no idea, when alone she simply drowned a teabag in a mug.

He hummed as he warmed, measured and stirred and she tried to focus on what to say to her brother. He had to understand the seriousness of her diagnosis but not be so alarmed that he became a gibbering wreck. She had to give him something positive to hold onto for his future without her, but what that could be, she had no idea. Thirty years ago, when their mother was dying in the hospice, Tina had made her a promise. So far, she had made no real effort to keep that promise – and now she'd left it too late. She remembered her mother's pleading face, pinched, anguished and grey with illness. The guilt of filial failure washed over her.

"Promise me, Tina, you'll see him happily settled down with a job and a nice girl?"

When he was younger Wayne had picked up casual labouring jobs but never stuck them for long. He couldn't stand the constant dirt on his hands. He'd managed a year of shop work when they still had a traditional ironmonger's in the town. The shop had closed in the face of competition from the new, giant DIY stores and the redundancy sapped what little confidence Wayne had. He gave up trying for work. As for nice girls – they were few and far between on the estate, especially ones that would consider going out with Wayne. As Tina made that promise, her mum's face and shoulders had visibly relaxed and she'd died at peace. Now it was nearing Tina's time to meet her mum again and to be held to account. Her conscience was pricking. It was unlikely she would get Wayne into work and married in the time she had left. Without either, his future situation was going to be difficult. Benefits weren't enough and Tina's cache of shop-lifting money had started to dwindle. In her weakened state it was impossible to contemplate hanging around department stores looking for a CCTV blackspot or waiting for an assistant to be distracted. And in a perfect world, as well as money, he would have the emotional support and guidance of a caring companion.

"You look done in, Sis." Wayne placed china mugs of tea on the small table between two armchairs, along with a couple of bourbon biscuits. Sitting down, he pushed one of the biscuits into his mouth.

"I've got something bad to tell you." She watched his jaws chew faster and waited for him to empty his mouth. He coughed on biscuit crumbs and took a drink of tea. "I've got terminal cancer." There was no point beating about the bush.

"Like Mum?" His voice trembled.

"Yes."

"No!" He stood up, his shins knocking the table and slopping tea on to its surface. For once the mess didn't bother him.

"They can't say how long I've got. I'll carry on having good days and bad days. I want to use the time I've got left to make sure you're all sorted for when I've gone." She released her breath: the facts were out and the subject turned to his future.

"I'll be all alone." The burst of anger had vanished and there were tears in his eyes. "They'll let me stay in the flat, won't they?"

"The council might expect you to move to a one-bedroom place."

She watched him look around the room. It wasn't much but it was all he'd ever known. Between them, they kept it clean, painted the walls every so often. The suite needed replacing but the carpet was only a year old and she'd be paying for it for another four years. Did the debt transfer to Wayne? She didn't know. The television was a big flat screen on the wall, also bought on credit, and the licence fee went out of the bank account by direct debit each month, along with the Sky money. How would Wayne manage all these outgoings?

His eyes were panicky and his lips were twisting. His forlorn expression tore at Tina's heart. She still had to explain the financial repercussions of her death. All her brother's memories and security were within these few rooms. He would fall apart if he had to move, even the familiarity of his rituals might not be enough to save him.

"You're too young to die," he said quietly.

She stood up, pulled him close and hugged him. Over the years Wayne had become more like her son than her brother. If she hadn't lost her baby in prison all those years ago, would she have loved that child any more than she loved Wayne? And it wasn't just her maternal feelings towards Wayne that made her feel responsible for his future – there was the guilt about that promise she'd made to her mother.

2

The three of them had the bridal shop to themselves. Olivia and her chief bridesmaid, Joanne, had negotiated extended lunch hours from work. Suzanne, Mark's sixteen-year-old daughter, had permission to be absent from school during her free period. The manager brought out the three full-length gowns that had been altered to fit. Olivia pulled rank as the bride and commandeered the single changing room first.

"Come out and give us a twirl!" called Joanne.

Olivia paused behind the heavy curtain of the cubicle and looked in the mirror. She needed a few moments before she became the focus of other people's comments. The dress fitted perfectly and made her feel young again, and attractive. She was on the cusp of a new life with a man she loved dearly. His love for her was obvious too in the little things he did: tea in bed each morning, a bunch of flowers when she least expected it, a willingness to share the cooking and the interest he took in all aspects of her life but without prying. Somehow she had managed to attract and keep this wonderful man whom she really didn't deserve. Her stomach fluttered with thrilled anticipation and the absolute certainty she was doing the right thing. That certainty had been absent in Las Vegas all those years ago. Back then pure impulsive excitement had driven her and Simon to tie the knot. They hadn't stopped to reflect or think. With the benefit of life experience and middle-age she could see they'd been two young, rootless things, trying to find their way without the stability or security of parents and family to anchor them, bound together by a terrible incident in their teenage years. Olivia carried the secret of that incident to this day – she was the only person left alive who knew the whole truth. It wasn't surprising she and Simon had clung to one another and tried to create a partnership for life. Neither was it a shock that their house-of-cards relationship had imploded when heaped with additional stress and grief so soon after their marriage.

This time around, with Mark, she'd be part of a mature partnership. They'd both been around the block and learned from it. They knew what to expect and would each work at making the other happy. Olivia's heart beat faster at the prospect of walking between pews full of smiling friends to reach Mark at the altar. She would shout 'I do!' loud enough for the whole world to hear.

"Are you alright in there?" Suzanne, Mark's daughter called. "You've not fainted or anything?"

Suzanne was another blessing Olivia didn't deserve. She and Simon had failed as parents and it was too late for her and Mark to have their own children but a share of Suzanne was the next best thing. Olivia had been reading step-parenting books like she once read baby magazines but Suzanne hadn't needed any kid glove treatment. The teenager had been more than happy to accept Olivia as her dad's girlfriend and they'd bonded over decorating one of Olivia's spare rooms for Suzanne to come and visit whenever she wanted. Already Mark lived at Olivia's almost permanently and after the wedding his smaller home would be sold. Olivia had given Suzanne a house key so she could drop off any posters and trinkets she wanted for personalising her room or just call in for a chat, even if her dad wasn't there.

"We're getting worried out here!" Joanne's voice held a hint of impatience. "You're not having second thoughts, are you? I don't want to lose what will probably be my last chance of ever being a bridesmaid."

Olivia pulled back the curtain and walked out into the main shop. There was a gasp and then a round of applause from Suzanne and Joanne.

"You look amazing."

"And your bum definitely does *not* look big in that."

The store manager circled Olivia, frowning, pulling at the fabric, then smoothing and patting it. "What do you think?" she asked the bride-to-be finally.

"It makes me feel fantastic. I could take on the world."

"That shows in your face," said Joanne. "You look radiant. Just as a bride should. Give me a tissue – I want to cry already."

Olivia twirled around and grinned. The shop manager directed first Suzanne and then Joanne into the cubicle to change into their bridesmaids' dresses.

Olivia crossed her fingers and hoped. A few months earlier Suzanne had been a reluctant member of the bridal party. She'd had a struggle with teenage puppy fat and had turned down Olivia's first request that she be a bridesmaid.

"I'll be all lumpy and bumpy in the photos," she'd said, prodding the extra flesh around her midriff and pulling a face. "Choose someone who won't break the camera."

"Oh, Suzanne! I want you as my bridesmaid because you're you! I want you to be part of my extremely important day – it's not a photo-shoot for *Hello* magazine. Please say yes?"

After some persuasion by both Olivia and Mark, Suzanne had relented and there'd been a long discussion with the store manager about which style of dress was going to work best. Now, as Suzanne stepped out of the changing room, Olivia noticed the usual little self-conscious hunch of her soon-to-be-stepdaughter's shoulders had disappeared and she was standing tall.

"This is brilliant. I've never worn a long dress before but now I understand the attraction." Suzanne turned around and around in front of the giant mirror on the shop floor. The silver-grey gown had been skilfully designed to hide the bumps and make her figure look sleek. "I'm going to wear this next summer to the sixth form prom – if that's alright?"

"Of course it is." Olivia gave her a hug and prayed the confidence created by this dress would stick around and replace some of the bad stuff that was going on in the girl's life. A few weeks previously, Suzanne had arrived unannounced and upset at Olivia's. She'd confided that a girl at school was making life difficult for her by continually prodding Suzanne's midriff and asking if that's where her family kept their cushions.

"That's bullying!" Olivia had been appalled. "We need to talk to the teacher."

"No! That will make it worse! I wish I hadn't told you now. You won't tell Dad, will you?"

Olivia had promised not to tell Mark or the school and since then she'd made an effort to find something complimentary to say every time she saw Suzanne. Neither of them had explicitly brought the subject up again but Olivia was trying to be hyper-aware of what might be going on in the girl's life. Some serious confidence-building was required.

When Suzanne vacated centre stage, Joanne stood perfectly still and gazed at her reflection. Then she turned to Olivia with a sad smile and eyes that blinked too quickly. "The last time I was in a shop like this was just before I married Roger…"

Olivia touched her friend's arm. "Roger would be so proud if he could see you now. You look stunning and he wouldn't want it any other way."

Olivia had thought twice about inviting her best friend to be a bridesmaid so soon after she'd lost her own husband. She was desperate to have Joanne's presence down the aisle but it had only been two years and she didn't want her friend to have a miserable time behind a fixed smile. Joanne always put on a brave face, however a wedding was bound to bring back memories more painful than usual.

"But what would he think about me starting a relationship with someone else? He'd hardly be proud of that. When I'm out with Simon I feel like I'm betraying Roger and all that we had between us."

Despite their differences, Olivia and her ex-husband Simon had remained on good terms after their divorce and she'd invited him to the engagement party six months earlier. She'd introduced him to Joanne and they'd clicked immediately. It felt like the old, fun Joanne was emerging again and that had cemented the decision to ask her to be part of the bridal party.

"You must never think that. When he was alive Roger encouraged you to follow your dreams. He never expected you to be the little wife at home. He'd still want you to make the most of everything and life is better when there's someone to share it with. Roger would be pleased to know that you're out meeting new people again."

Joanne smoothed down the front of her gown. "I have to believe you or I'd throw myself in the canal."

"I'd never let you do that. Whenever you feel so bad – call me!"

The manager finished circling and tweaking Joanne and Suzanne. "If you're all happy with the fitting I'll get these dresses packaged up and you can take them away with you."

In turn they disrobed from their fairy tale frocks and stepped back into the real life attire of office and college. The dresses were boxed up and put in the boot of Olivia's car. The countdown to the big day had begun.

***

Suzanne had to stop herself skipping like a small excited kid as she made her way back to school. The dress had turned out tons better than she'd expected and made her feel like some glamourous model on a photo shoot. When she looked in the mirror she hadn't believed how wonderful it made her look. And how wonderful it made her feel.

She slowed down when the college came into sight. As usual there were lads sitting on the wall, smoking and laughing. She knew a couple of them from school, they'd left last year after GCSEs to do stuff like plumbing and bricklaying at the college. She usually crossed the road at this point to avoid whatever stupid comments they might shout at her. But that dress had given her an injection of confidence. There was no reason for her to take the long way around. She'd walk past them in the way she'd walked around the bridal shop and see what they made of that.

Focus on how you looked in that mirror, she told herself as she drew level with the first youth. She put her head up, her shoulders back and pretended she was on a catwalk in a long silver gown. The first boy was chewing gum and absorbed in his phone. The next two gave her an appreciative whistle which made her blush but built her confidence even further.

"Hey, Suzanne!" the last lad called after her.

It was Dean Waddington. She'd recognised him before she even got to where the boys were sitting and he was the one she was most nervous of. At school all the other girls had fancied him like mad but he'd barely acknowledged her existence. He had a reputation for being as hard as nails. Should she turn round to face him and take the inevitable insults or should she scurry away?

She turned round and smiled. "Hi, Dean."

"You changed your hair or something? You look different."

"No. Nothing's changed." Her heart was bumping and any minute now he'd make some sarcastic comment about her burning red cheeks. She braced herself.

"Sit down." He patted the empty bit of wall next to him.

For a second she wondered if she'd misheard.

"It's clean," he said. "I've brushed the bird crap off."

Hardly daring to believe it, she sat down. He offered her a cigarette. She refused. He offered her a piece of chewing gum and she accepted. Was this really happening to her? The boy who'd been the heartthrob of Year 11 was paying attention to her? It was as though wearing that dress had left her covered in magical fairy dust.

"So, how's it going?" He took a puff on the cigarette and breathed deeply.

"Good. Things are going good. In a few weeks it'll be the summer holidays and then things will be even better." She remembered school and looked at her watch. If she didn't go now she'd miss the beginning of the next period and that hadn't been part of the deal when she'd been given special permission to go out. She stood up. "I'll be seeing ya. Thanks for the gum."

"School?"

She nodded.

"One lesson won't make no difference." He took her hand and pulled gently. "Stay here with me. We never really talked to each other before, did we?"

Weird sensations were travelling up her arm and through her body. She felt slightly breathless and he was still holding her hand. The other lads had disappeared. Any minute now the Maths lesson would start but perhaps they wouldn't even realise she was missing. Which was more important, Maths or Dean Waddington holding her hand?

"Got me driving test next month," he said. "Dad says I can borrow 'is car after that. As soon as I'm working I'll get me own."

"I've only had four lessons." It got more amazing – they had something in common to talk about!

"I've 'ad fifteen total and practice with me dad."

Dean held her hand and they talked for a whole hour. Then he had to go and they swapped mobile numbers. Suzanne went home feeling invincible.

3

Since Tina had told him the bad news Wayne had started treating her with kid gloves. Under her supervision he willingly did all the cooking and cleaning. Housework became his forte and he spent three hours every morning cleaning the flat throughout. He wouldn't allow a dirty mug to sit in the sink – it had to be washed, dried and put away. Tina followed him around wishing she could channel his energy into a paid job that would make him financially secure.

This morning the vacuum cleaner crashed against a cupboard door in Tina's bedroom, the door flew open and a pile of papers spewed out. Wayne hit the off switch as the first page reacted to the strong suction of the cleaner.

He bent down and gathered up the sheets. "They're just old letters. I'll bin them."

"No! Let me look first." She recognised the curling, yellowing papers as letters she'd received in prison. They were mostly from her mum. Wayne might like some of them as a souvenir but they needed sorting first. She left Wayne to his vacuum and feather duster, carried the letters into the lounge and curled up on the sofa.

The slanted, looped writing in blue biro on cheap paper

brought tears to Tina's eyes. Her mum described how she was holding down an early morning cleaning job and regular evening shifts in a supermarket to make ends meet. Tina had never been able to match her mother's work ethic and she knew her mum would be disappointed if she knew how Tina had turned out. When she'd first been released Tina had tried to make an honest living. The cleaning firm her mum worked for had taken her on but the work wasn't pleasant. The company specialised in contract cleaning for the pubs in the area that weren't yet part of the growing national chains. The work had to be done in the mornings before the pubs opened for business at lunchtime and there was nothing inviting about an empty bar seen in the harsh morning light. The bonhomie of customers and staff was absent, a dank smell of stale smoke and alcohol hung in the air, the nicotine stained walls and ceilings looked neglected and the stains on the carpet were plainly visible as the hoover went up and down. But the toilets were the worst. They were often left unflushed or blocked. Sometimes punters didn't make it as far as the toilet meaning there was usually vomit to clean up. Tina's respect for her mother grew; to put up with this year after year required a special strength of character.

"When you've kids to feed, you do whatever it takes to put food on the table," her mum had said. "If there was absolutely no alternative, I suppose I'd even sell my body. If you had children…"

Her mother's voice had tailed off and Tina knew she'd suddenly remembered her daughter's miscarriage in prison. Tina knew too that if her baby had lived she would've also worked herself silly to give it the best of everything. But she'd never been blessed with that precious incentive. Perhaps if she had, she wouldn't have given up the cleaning job as soon as her mother was buried in order to take up easier, less legal ways to make cash – a move that would have horrified her mother.

Now, knowing she was about to die, there wasn't much time

for a last-ditch attempt to make her mum proud. But if she could sort something out for Wayne that might be enough to ease her conscience for when she met Mum again in whatever afterlife was waiting for her.

Tina picked up an envelope with writing she didn't recognise. The lettering was prouder and more confident than her mother's, not so old-fashioned and self-effacing. There was no address, just the names 'Simon and Olivia'. The envelope was sealed and the names vaguely familiar. Tina went backwards through time trying unsuccessfully to turn the names into real people. Then she used her finger under the envelope flap to open it. It contained a thick sheet of paper folded in half. In the top right corner of the letter was the name of the prison where Tina had spent her last jail term and a date in 1986. She began to read:

Dear Simon and Olivia,

The person bearing this letter is my cellmate, Tina Mallinson. She's been a source of great friendship and guidance for me in here. Now she's paid her dues to society and is a free woman. She keeps an eye on her younger brother, Wayne, because their mother has to work long hours. He's the same age as you two. Tina has very kindly offered to be there if either of you need help in my absence. In return, if ever Tina or Wayne requires help I have promised that you will provide that assistance. Please keep that promise for me. It's a hard world and we all have to stick together.

Lots of Love
Mum
XXXXX

Now Tina remembered. It was the day before she was released from her last prison term. Her cellmate, Audrey, was inside for murdering her violent husband. She wasn't the prison kind, she wasn't streetwise and had no concept of anything that wasn't law-abiding. She would've had a hell of a time if Tina hadn't befriended her. Audrey probably didn't realise it, but this friendship hadn't been a selfless act on Tina's part. Prison requires the wearing of a 'hard' mask and, if you drop that artificial shield in front of the wrong person, you make yourself vulnerable to all sorts of bullying and ill-treatment. Tina was struggling to maintain that front but with Audrey she didn't even have to try and their relationship became a safety-valve.

She could tell Audrey about the first time she'd been put away. It had been for receiving stolen property and her then boyfriend had talked her into it. She'd come into prison pregnant and the stress of the hard, alien environment had made her lose the baby. No one had seemed to care and she hadn't been able to talk to anyone inside about it. So everything had just gone round and round in her brain, building up to a head of steam like a pressure cooker. All that steam erupted when she was released. She stole a baby. Just wheeled the pram away from a children's playground whilst the mother was busy pushing her other kids on the swings. Even now, Tina could remember justifying her actions to herself. The woman had more children than she could look after properly and the baby in the pram was being neglected. Looking back it was obvious that taking the baby had been wrong, but at the time she'd thought she would give that child a much better life than its birth mother ever could with so many other kids running around the place. The police had caught up with Tina before nightfall and there'd been medical reports done by doctors but still she'd been incarcerated again. And that's when she'd met Audrey.

Audrey had insisted Tina should 'go straight' on her next release. "I really don't want to see you back in here," she'd said.

"You're not stupid, if you put the effort in you could do so much better for yourself. You've got an innate intelligence that will serve you well in any job. I promise you that whatever help you need, my son Simon and his girlfriend, Olivia will give it to you. One good turn deserves another and you've been brilliant to me in here."

That's when Audrey had written the letter and given it to her.

"I'll be back," Tina had teased, "but only to visit you."

Back at the flat, with her mum, brother and new cleaning job, Tina had stuffed the letter away and forgotten about it. She had kept her word and visited Audrey, but only sporadically with a growing number of months between each visit. On her last visit, a year after her release, there'd been a couple of other visitors waiting for Audrey. They'd introduced themselves as Audrey's son and his girlfriend. She'd forgotten their names but they must have been Olivia and Simon. Shortly after that Audrey had committed suicide in prison, Tina's mum had died and Tina became a master shoplifter rather than work for a living.

Now she re-read the letter to Simon and Olivia and wondered whether it was too late to call in this promised favour – for Wayne's sake rather than her own.

***

"Get away!" The middle-aged woman in the fussy blouse was pulling Olivia away from the body. "I'll fix it. Don't touch anything else."

In response Olivia stumbled backwards and cowered in a corner still trying to wipe the blood from her hands. An image of Lady Macbeth in a white nightdress with long, dark, wild hair superimposed itself on the retro hallway. She was staring at her red-stained, upturned hands and screeching in a Kate Bush type wail. "What, will these hands ne'er been clean?" And then Lady Macbeth morphed into Olivia's O' level English teacher.

When Olivia started to giggle from her corner in the hallway, the teacher disappeared and the woman in the blouse was back bending over the body. She was wearing an apron around her waist and used it to wipe the handle of the knife as it protruded from the man's body. She wiped it thoroughly several times as though desperate to remove an incriminating mark. Then she placed both hands on the handle and looked as though she was about to pull it from the body.

"No!" Simon shouted from the stairs.

Olivia jumped with shock. The woman moved back from the prone man.

"You'll make it worse if you remove the knife. He might be still alive." Simon jumped the last few stairs and then bent over the body next to the woman.

Then Simon and the woman both stood up. This must be what a massacre looked like – everyone covered in the blood of the dead, or the nearly dead. Olivia started to shake. This was the nearest she'd ever been to death. She pulled her knees up to her chest and rocked in her corner of the hallway.

Simon called the emergency services. Mesmerised, Olivia watched his fingers twist the cream curled cord and turn it the prettiest shade of pink.

The sirens didn't come this time but the police did. Four of them stormed the front door and grabbed Olivia from her corner. She screamed. The woman in the blouse yelled they'd got the wrong person. "The fingerprints on the knife are mine!" she screamed.

Simon tried to pull Olivia from the clutches of the police but they dragged her out of the house and threw her into the back of a police van. She screamed again. The blood was all over her clothes, marking her out as the guilty party. As the van accelerated away she was thrown around the bare, metallic interior.

Then she was half-awake and screaming.

"Hush. Hush." Mark was holding her.

"Let me go. It's a mistake. Let me go. She said she'd sort it out. She wiped my fingerprints. There's no evidence."

Mark wouldn't release her arms. He just kept reassuring her in a quiet voice. Eventually she calmed down and he loosened his grip.

"Same dream?" he asked.

"Worse. Much worse." She was clinging to him now instead of trying to break free. "The police took me away. The police have never taken me away before." She was shivering as the sweat dried on her body.

"Perhaps you should have some counselling," Mark said gently. "It might get to the trigger of the dreams and switch them off."

"No! I don't need counselling. I'm not mentally ill. I just get bad dreams. Lots of people have bad dreams. It's no big deal." She couldn't go to counselling – it was too big a risk. Too much might spill out of her. Already she might have told Mark too much.

"It is a big deal when they start happening with increasing frequency and leave you exhausted the next day. And they leave me exhausted."

"It's the stress of the wedding. Lots of women have weird dreams in the lead up to the wedding. It says so in the bridal magazines."

"I've read those too and the dreams are about walking down the aisle naked or in a tatty homemade dress. They are not dreams about witnessing a murder and being covered in the victim's blood. Or being carted off by the police."

"If I relax a bit more I'll be OK. I'm just too hyped up at the moment." Olivia wanted to distract them both from the terrifying content of the dreams. She shouldn't have told him the detail but such vivid fear in the middle of the night loosened her tongue. She needed to change the subject. "Let's go out for dinner tomorrow night with Simon and Joanne. That'll take my mind off things."

She'd thought the nightmares were a thing of her past. They'd been frequent in her late teens and early twenties. Her parents put it down to what she'd witnessed and decided she'd grow out of it. They'd been sort of right. The dreams had eased off after Simon's mother committed suicide – as though that had been the end of a chapter. Shortly after that David had been born and other dramas had taken over her life. These had ultimately been treated successfully with anti-depressants. But the dreams had returned with a vengeance about a month ago. Mark had been frightened the first time she'd woken up screaming. He'd wanted to call a doctor. It had taken great effort on Olivia's part to get herself under control and calm Mark. Since then he'd got better at dealing with it but she was afraid he'd do something stupid like arrange a counselling session she couldn't get out of.

"Dinner would be great," Joanne said when Olivia called the next morning. "Simon will be pleased too. He likes Mark, thinks he's good for you."

Olivia smiled. Despite their failure to remain married, she and Simon had a special bond. Until Joanne started going out with him, they didn't see each other regularly but he was like the big brother she'd never had and always there if she needed him. Simon was a good person to have on side.

Simon and Joanne were already at the table when Mark and Olivia arrived at the restaurant. They were holding hands and laughing – 'the perfect couple' was the only way to describe them. On occasion, Olivia thought Simon was better suited to Joanne than her friend's first husband had been.

"Olivia's been having bad dreams," Mark announced once the waiter had poured the wine and taken their food order.

"Mark!" Olivia frowned in disapproval at her fiancé. She would've attempted a kick under the table if there wasn't a risk that she'd hit Simon instead. "That's hardly the most pleasant dinner conversation and I thought the aim of coming out tonight was to forget about all that nastiness. Not to dwell on it."

"Sorry but these two people are closer to you than anyone else. If there's some concrete foundation for the nightmares they might be able to shed some light on it. We can't go on waking in the early hours, night after night. It's exhausting."

Simon and Joanne shifted in their seats. It was obvious they felt uncomfortable.

"Probably just pre-wedding nerves," Joanne said lightly. "It happened to me when I married Roger. Every night for weeks I dreamt that when I put my wedding dress on it had shrunk into a mini-skirt that barely covered my bottom. I refused to wear it and walked down the aisle in my dressing gown instead. As soon as the wedding was over the dreams stopped."

"That I could understand," said Mark. "But in Olivia's dream she's the witness to a murder."

Simon's eyes flicked towards her but his expression didn't change. Joanne looked interested. Olivia stared down at the cutlery in front of her.

"It's in the hallway of a house and from the décor and fashion we think it must be 1980s," Mark continued. "A man's lying on the floor, stabbed. There's blood everywhere and screaming. Someone calls the police. Olivia always mentions how the telephone cord turns pink with the blood on the caller's fingers – as though that's an important detail. Then there's sirens and Olivia wakes up screaming and wakes me up too. Any ideas?"

The silence went on too long. Simon stared at the starched cream napkin in front of him. Joanne was playing with her soup spoon and casting glances at Simon as though trying to get his permission to speak.

"Have I said something wrong?" Mark was looking round at them all.

"No, as I said, just the wrong subject for a pleasant dinner."

Olivia unfolded a piece of A4 paper on the table. "How about giving me some help with this seating plan?"

"Those dreams don't just affect you, Olivia. They affect me too. By the time we get married I'm going to be an exhausted wreck and they scared Suzanne when she stayed last weekend."

"We might be able to help," Joanne said tentatively, glancing at Simon again.

Olivia tried to use her eyes and facial expression to tell her friend to shut up. But Joanne was still looking at Simon.

"Did you know that Simon's father was murdered in their hallway in the early 1980s? Olivia was a witness and Simon came down the stairs immediately afterwards."

"Oh my God! Simon, I'm so sorry. I had no idea."

"That's OK. It's not something I broadcast." The spoon he was fiddling with clattered to the floor. He bent down and retrieved it. "It's on a need-to-know basis I suppose. Joanne and I were becoming closer so I felt she needed to know."

"Well that explains the nightmares. Olivia, why on earth didn't you tell me about all this?"

Olivia shrugged. "No disrespect to Simon's mother but it was a long time ago and I don't want to spend my whole life being labelled as 'the girl who witnessed a murder.'"

The waiter brought the starters and the conversation halted whilst rolls were buttered and everyone made appreciative noises about the dishes put in front of them.

"Did they catch who did it?" Mark asked.

"Yes, it was my mother. She committed suicide a few years later in prison."

"I don't know what to say."

"No need to say anything. He was a violent bastard who had it coming to him. Now shall we talk about Olivia's seating plan?"

The tension eased slowly as they discussed the relative merits of who should sit where.

"The big problem is where to seat my ex-wife," Mark

said. "Suzanne wants her mum to come and see her in all her bridesmaid finery but she won't know a soul. And it's not a good conversation opener if she introduces herself as the groom's first wife."

"I'll look after her," Simon offered. "Being the bride's first husband is equally embarrassing and I'll be on my tod with Joanne on the top table."

"Great." Olivia made a final note on her paper, folded it and slipped it in her handbag. "Now, dare we have a pudding knowing that we've got those dresses to fit into?"

They were in bed when Mark brought up the subject of the dreams again. "You knew what was causing those dreams. Why didn't you tell me?"

"People react differently. Some heap sympathy on me as though I was the victim and others want to know all the gory details from what the blood smelt like to whether being a real witness in a real court is anything like on the TV. I don't like either of those reactions so I never volunteer any information. I don't like talking about it – full stop. If it makes you feel any better, I never told Joanne either. She only found out through Simon – and, like you, she played hell with me afterwards."

"Is there anything else you haven't told me?"

Olivia hesitated. "No." There was some information you could never volunteer to anyone.

4

Tina pulled the letter out of the envelope again. It was becoming dog-eared she'd looked at it so many times, trying to figure out how, or even if, she could use it to get help for Wayne. She was feeling more tired these days and she didn't always think clearly. She had to go over things two or three times in her mind to make sure she was being realistic. Most of all Wayne needed a steady income but this couple, Simon and Olivia, were unlikely to agree to give him money. They had no reason to help in any way now that Audrey, Simon's mother, was long since dead. Unless the couple felt the promise in the letter should be honoured on moral grounds, regardless of whether Audrey was still around to check up on them.

Tina held the letter between her thumb and forefinger and pondered, running her thumb up and down the edge of the paper. The sensation between the two digits changed and Tina realised she wasn't holding one thick sheet of paper but two thin sheets. She peeled the second sheet away from the letter expecting it to be blank and torn off the writing pad in error. A small amount of adhesive gum along the top edge of the sheets had been holding them together. The second sheet wasn't blank. It was a page of writing entitled 'Getting It off My

Chest'. It took a couple of seconds for Tina to realise it must have been a homework exercise for Audrey. In the prison they were constantly encouraged to go to 'Writing for Therapy' classes. Tina always refused. She could read but writing her own words had never been a strong point and she didn't want to show herself up. Olivia went religiously and always scribbled furiously when she came back to the cell. Much of it got torn up and thrown away. Tina guessed the therapy bit was in getting the words down on paper, not in reading them back or showing them to anyone else. This looked like one bit of therapy that hadn't got thrown away. Tina wondered if she should tear the page up and bin it – it hadn't been written for public consumption. But her eyes were drawn to the words:

Getting It off My Chest

I didn't murder my husband. Much as I wanted him dead, I didn't stab him that day. I wish I had – it would have done wonders for my self-esteem. Somebody else took the initiative and did it for me. I'm grateful but it's left me feeling useless – a young girl did, in a split second, what I didn't have the nerve to do during all those years of abusive marriage. There'd been plenty of opportunity for me to kill him. He was a heavy sleeper, I could've stabbed him as he slept. Or I could have laced his food with my sleeping pills – he ate at speed, hardly tasting anything. I fantasised about sending him to his grave but I never had the courage to follow it through. It took a young girl to show me what I should've done years ago. He'd been abusing me for a long time. At first I didn't realise it was abuse because it wasn't physical. It was controlling: stuff like not giving me enough housekeeping money, not letting me drive the car, refusing to let me go to the hairdressers more than a couple of times a year. Then, more recently, if he'd had a bad day at work he'd thump me when he got home. He'd just walk into the kitchen where I was cooking, punch me in the stomach and then walk out again – all without saying a word. A couple of days before he died I dropped a glass on the kitchen floor. It smashed on the tiles. I bent to pick up the pieces and he kicked me so hard I landed in the glass shards.

When the police took me in after Frank's murder I was able to show them all the cuts and bruises and plead that it was self-defence. Olivia couldn't have done that. She wouldn't have had a leg to stand on. That's why, when she lunged at him with that knife, she was so much braver than I ever could be. If the police had got hold of her she would have gone down for life and she didn't deserve that. She deserved a medal. I owe my life to Olivia. If she hadn't killed him, he would most certainly have killed me one day very soon. I'm not glad I'm in prison but I deserve it for my cowardice. It's the only thing I can do to thank Olivia Field for what she did – I can keep her out of jail. I want her and Simon to have the chance of a good future together – that's what they deserve.

Audrey had signed and dated the piece of writing. It had definitely been included in the envelope by mistake.

Tina read the passage three times. In all the time they'd spent together, Audrey had never even hinted that she was an innocent woman. How could she be so brave? Tina remembered lying in the narrow bunk above Audrey and the many conversations they had about their lives on the outside. She knew all about Frank's abuse and Audrey knew all about Tina's life in the tower block, the miscarriage and how it had messed with her head. Audrey had never said she was in prison for something she didn't do. It was all a very long time ago. Tina closed her eyes and put herself back in that prison cell. The walls were light grey emulsion. There were splashes of colour where they'd fastened up family photos and postcards. There was the desk and chair where Audrey scribbled away after the creative writing class. The small window had bars and a view over a concrete yard if you stood on tiptoe. Tina tried to concentrate on what they'd talked about. Now she remembered Audrey mentioning Olivia as her son's girlfriend and she was included in the letter Audrey had given her but she'd never been mentioned in conjunction with the killing. Audrey's innocence was news to Tina.

In prison Tina had pitied Audrey. She'd been dropped into a hostile environment where she'd been bait for the vultures. Audrey didn't have the background to cope inside but Tina's friendship had saved her. Now Audrey suddenly rose up on a pedestal. She'd never squealed on Olivia and had taken her punishment without a murmur – even though it drove her to suicide. Not like some of the others who swore they were innocent even though there was a crate load of concrete evidence against them.

Olivia must still be wandering around free as a bird. What would happen if the police saw what Audrey had written? They would know Olivia had stabbed Frank and Audrey had covered up for her. They would know Olivia should've gone to prison and not Audrey. If the police saw this piece of paper they would arrest Olivia on the spot.

Tina began to tremble with excitement. How much would Olivia pay for this not to fall into the hands of the cops? Had Simon known about this deception all along? Could he be done as part of a conspiracy to pervert the course of justice? A way of securing Wayne's future was materialising before Tina's eyes. In her letter, Audrey had promised Simon and Olivia would help Tina on the outside. Tina now had the means to make sure they kept that promise and gave her an extremely large amount of help.

Tina's conscience started whispering. A true friend would not do this. Audrey wouldn't like it if she knew Tina was going to bulldoze into Simon and Olivia's lives and start blackmailing them. But it wouldn't be wrong to give them a chance at helping her via the letter of introduction first. If they had morals they would, even at this late date, keep Audrey's promise. If they refused they deserved everything they had coming to them. Even if that included blackmail.

Tina's social media and internet search skills were zero. But the estate held plenty of teenagers willing to help her out for a few bottles of cider and some cigarettes. They couldn't track down home addresses but it didn't take long for the youths to produce places of work for Simon Frome and Olivia Field.

***

Olivia took the train into Birmingham city centre every day. She used to drive but spiralling car park charges and the increasing time spent in jams made rail transport more and more attractive. It still wasn't pleasant – in the morning, the train was often full by the time it arrived at Sutton Coldfield and Olivia had to stand squashed like a sardine. It was odd to be pressed so close to these people physically but also to be completely ignored by them on a social level. Everyone stared at the floor, the ceiling, the door, down the carriage, at a phone, anywhere that didn't risk making eye contact with the mass of uncomfortable, impatient humanity around them. Tinny sounds escaped from tiny white headphones plugged into dozens of ears. The only people who spoke or interacted in anyway with their fellow man were the teenagers dressed, to varying degrees of smartness, in school uniform. These youngsters, so often accused of being addicted to electronic devices to the exclusion of all social interaction, were the ones gossiping, swapping homework notes and even pertinent observations on the day's headlines.

Generally the journey home was better. When the train

from Longbridge arrived at New Street Station it disgorged 95% of its passengers leaving plenty of empty seats for those making the homeward journey to north Birmingham – except for those commuters who had to sprint down the platform at the last minute to squeeze on before the guard sent the train on its way. The first passengers onto the train all chose separate seats, marking out their territory with handbags, laptops or jackets on the adjacent seat in the hope that no one would choose to sit next to them. These passengers knew it was a futile gesture because the train would be full by the time it pulled out of the station but they did it anyway.

Olivia was no exception. She sat down on the window seat and placed her handbag and jacket on the aisle seat. Then she got out her phone. Work emails were still arriving in her inbox. She glanced at the subject lines, nothing urgent. Thank goodness. Her shoulders relaxed and she closed her eyes. There'd been a difficult client meeting immediately after lunch where she'd had to apologise for the cock-up made by a member of her team when implementing a new software release. Somewhere along the line the testing hadn't been sufficiently thorough and one of the new programs had failed in the client's live computer environment, causing them a lot of manual work to put it right. The client had accepted the apology but now Olivia would have to be on red alert to make sure her team knew no further mistakes would be tolerated. All newly written software must work perfectly.

"Excuse me, do you mind if I sit 'ere?" It was a female voice.

Olivia opened her eyes. The woman's face was thin and pale. She wore a mustard skirt and jacket that had once been in fashion. Couldn't she see there were still plenty of whole double empty seats around? Why would anyone choose to share when it wasn't necessary? Reluctantly, Olivia moved the handbag and jacket from the adjacent seat onto her lap and went back to her phone. Every time the train stopped, Olivia hoped the woman would get off so that she could reclaim her space. The woman didn't get off until Sutton Coldfield, with Olivia. In summer Olivia walked home across Sutton Park, in winter she drove to the station. Today Olivia walked out of the car park past the closed up kiosk where the chatty attendant collected money in the mornings.

She entered the park at Town Gate and there were still children running around the playground. A group of mums stood gossiping. A sudden blast of music battered her from behind and she turned to see a scarlet, souped-up Fiesta with windows down perform a handbrake turn. Olivia couldn't stop her head shaking in disapproval. At that moment she noticed the woman in mustard again. She was about ten feet behind Olivia and their eyes met. Olivia looked away quickly. There was something about the woman that was vaguely familiar. She didn't know where or when she'd seen her before but she was getting a bad feeling.

Olivia quickened her step. The weather was warm and, despite it being the end of the day, the ford through the stream at Wyndley Gate was full of children paddling. Dogs were running in and out of the water and shaking themselves indiscriminately over anyone unfortunate enough to be near. Olivia side-stepped to avoid a soggy black and white collie. At the same time she glanced over her shoulder, the woman in mustard was taking the same route through the park as her. She was still there but further behind when Olivia exited the park at Boldmere Gate and walked up the hill to the roundabout. That bad feeling was still hovering and Olivia was now walking quicker than usual and beginning to sweat. She glanced behind again, the gap between her and the woman had widened. The rush hour traffic was busy on Monmouth Drive and Olivia had to wait several minutes to cross the road, allowing the woman to catch up. They crossed side by side but without acknowledging each other and then Olivia took the lead again. She walked straight up her garden path without looking behind. Inside the house she leant against the closed front door, took a deep breath and reprimanded herself for getting uptight over nothing. In the summer loads of people walked across the park from the station. That one particular woman should sit next to her on the train and then walk the same route home was nothing to be concerned about. She probably lived further down the road and that's why she was familiar.

Olivia walked into the lounge and looked out of the window. The woman was stood on the pavement writing something down. She looked up and met Olivia's eye. Olivia shuddered and let the net curtain fall.

"A woman followed me home today," she told Mark when he got back from work. "She was wearing a mustard suit."

"What do you mean followed?" He kissed her as she stirred bacon in the frying pan for carbonara

"Whenever I looked round, there she was. And she paused outside our house and wrote something down."

"Probably just a coincidence. Are you going to pour the wine or shall I?"

The next day Olivia deliberately left work forty minutes later so that she and the woman wouldn't be on the same train. The pavement crush outside the office building had thinned by this time and, as soon as the automatic glass doors opened for her, Olivia saw the mustard jacket and skirt looking in a shop window fifty feet in the direction Olivia had to walk to the station. Olivia deliberately crossed the road and walked on the opposite pavement. The woman moved in parallel with her. They entered the station within feet of each other. Olivia took the escalator to the wrong platform on purpose. The woman followed. Olivia came back up the escalator and went into the Ladies toilet. She locked herself in a cubicle and waited ten minutes. When she came out the woman in mustard was combing her hair in front of the mirror. Olivia noticed the woman's hair was very thin and large amounts were coming out in the teeth of the comb.

They'd met before, Olivia was sure, but she didn't know where or when. It wasn't recently. She wanted to say something to the woman. She took a deep breath but no words came. Then she told herself that talking might encourage this stalker, if that's what she was. If she wasn't a stalker and it was all coincidence, saying something would make Olivia look like a mad woman.

This time the woman sat across the aisle from Olivia on the train. It was a later train and emptier so Olivia got up and chose a different seat down the other end of the carriage. The woman followed. Now Olivia was certain the woman was following her. She was in no danger on the train because there were other people around but walking through the park as evening fell might not be so wise. Olivia called Mark and asked him to pick her up from the station.

"I'm running late," she said and then lowered her voice. "And the woman who followed me yesterday is on the train again." She glanced up to see if the woman had heard but she was staring out of the window.

Mark was waiting in the car park with the engine running.

"There she is." Olivia pulled the passenger door shut behind her and tilted her head to indicate the woman. She was only ten feet away and staring at the car.

"She looks frail and harmless."

"She gives me the creeps and there's no doubt she's following me. And I'm sure I know her from somewhere."

"You're exaggerating. You've probably seen her everyday on the train for weeks but never really noticed her properly before."

5

They were married! Everything had gone without a hitch. The organist began Mendelssohn's Wedding March and Mark gently took Olivia's arm. The butterflies in her stomach had gone and her whole body felt infused with joy. Out of the corner of her eye she could see the best man take Joanne's arm and Suzanne was getting ready to process with the usher. She looked up at Mark, his dark eyes were tender and all she could see in his face was love. She stood on tiptoe and kissed him. A cheer went up from the front pews. Olivia felt herself blush. Then they walked down the aisle through a cacophony of rousing organ music, clapping and good luck wishes. When they reached the church doorway they posed for a photograph and then the bells started ringing. She thought her heart would burst with happiness. Guests were getting ready to shower them with confetti and Olivia looked down to check her bouquet. She wanted Joanne to catch it.

She screamed. The red roses had been replaced with a kitchen knife coated in red blood. The blood was fresh and steaming. It was dripping from the knife onto the pure white silk of her dress, turning it pink. Pink like the curled telephone cord.

Olivia's screams wouldn't stop. Then Mark was holding

her close. She buried her face in his chest. Then pulled back, she didn't want to get tears and blood on his wedding suit. But he wouldn't let her go and his chest was bare. The church and the guests were gone, replaced by the familiar dark shapes of bedroom chair, wardrobe and dressing table.

"I really do think you should go for counselling," Mark whispered. "I know all this was triggered by your bad experience as a teenager but you can't let it blight both our lives into the future. Having the same nightmare this frequently just isn't normal and neither is suspecting perfectly innocent women of stalking you."

"I can't go for counselling!" Olivia banged her fist on Mark's chest. A counsellor would dredge up all the bad stuff from her past. Stuff that had to stay hidden. Stuff that Olivia had never stopped feeling guilty for. "Eventually it will go away by itself, it did before."

***

The sound of voices and a door banging woke Tina. She looked at the clock, it was 3am.

"Wayne?"

"Wait there and I'll get you what I can. She's usually got cash in the place."

Tina winced. He was going to take more of her depleted shoplifting cash. He just didn't get the concept of saving money for the future. Too many times in recent months her brother had taken great chunks of her ready cash to pay off his gambling debts. His so-called 'mates' took advantage of his naïve nature when they were in need of money and he never failed to deliver. He seemed unable to win any game of cards. Wayne walked into her bedroom and turned on the light. She sat up blinking.

"Is your purse 'andy, Sis? I owe a bit of money."

"We can't go on like this, Wayne. I can't keep bailing you out. What will happen when I'm gone?"

He hesitated a second before continuing. "Fifty quid, that's all I need. You must have that much. It's the last time, I promise."

"You always say that."

"We ain't got all day, Wayne." The voice from the hallway was impatient and aggressive.

Tina was too tired to argue. She pointed to her handbag. Wayne gave her a thumbs up and counted out the notes loudly. He was considerate enough to turn out the light and close the door when he went back into the hallway. Tina struggled to relax and find sleep again. Sometimes she felt death was almost upon her and it would be a blessed relief. She'd done her best to look after Wayne but he was a grown man with a will of his own. A lot of the time he was thoughtful and cooperative but other times he went his own way. She suspected he was lonely and would do anything to be allowed to be part of 'the gang'. But the gang never made any allowance for him and his needs. The gambling crowd wasted large chunks of his time and benefit money in card games. He always thought the next time he'd win big and had promised Tina cruises, cars and even a house. He didn't have the intellect to realise even if he won, the chances of the win being sizable were nil. In the meantime he was taken advantage of by people who always knew they could beat him.

At times she wanted to disown him but then she thought of the baby she'd lost and the life she would've wanted for him. Audrey had written about the ultimate sacrifice she'd made for the future she hoped Simon would have with Olivia. Her mum had wanted Wayne to have the best life possible and it was now down to Tina to make it happen. She had the beginnings of a plan but if Olivia and Simon weren't cooperative she wasn't sure how she'd follow it through. Everyone she knew muddled through life at the bottom of the pile, some more law-abiding than others but none getting above the dizzy heights of temporary labouring jobs or cleaning on the industrial estate.

The smoke alarm burst into life. Tina jumped.

"Not for real. It's only me, Sis! Don't panic!"

Tina pulled the duvet over her head. If he had to make toast at this time of night he could at least watch it didn't burn. The toilet flushed. The tap ran at full throttle. Then stopped, then ran again. She counted seven times that Wayne filled the washbasin and washed his hands. Ever since their mother's death all those years ago he'd become obsessed with what disaster might befall them next. For Wayne, following a strict routine with repetitive rituals was the only way the disaster would be averted. His obsession stretched to food too. If she bought the wrong brand of beans he couldn't eat anything at all until the correct brand had been bought and consumed. He'd even painted a line around the bottom of his mug to show how much milk should go in before his tea. When she'd dropped her handbag mirror on the kitchen floor and it'd smashed, he'd gone mad.

"That's seven years bad luck for both of us," he'd shouted and taken to his bed for four days until Tina refused to serve any more meals in his room.

Maybe he was right about the bad luck because it was shortly after that that the cough had started. Unfortunately his rituals and obsessions wouldn't be able to stop the inevitable. Wayne's bedroom door closed and then there was silence. It was four am. No wonder neither of them could keep the hours that a 'proper' job demanded.

The next day Tina felt bad, really bad. They'd told her at the hospital that things could go up and down.

"Take care of yourself. Don't try to do too much," they'd said.

It was easy for them to say. They weren't responsible for Wayne, his often upside down body clock and ensuring that he'd be able to manage in the future. Tina had to act before she was bedridden or in a hospice. Audrey had played on her mind a lot over the last few days and Tina knew what she was planning was far beyond what Audrey had meant when she made the promise of help from Simon and Olivia. But, at the end of the day, blood was thicker than water and she had to do what was best for Wayne. She felt like a lioness willing to fight to the death to protect her cub. Even so, she was going to go softly, softly at first. There was no point getting people's backs up if it wasn't necessary.

She approached Simon directly first by phoning the estate agents where he worked. She explained that she'd been close friends with his mother in prison and had a letter that might interest him. Best to let him think that there might be something in the meeting for him rather than alienate him with threats over the phone. She suggested he bring Olivia and they meet for coffee.

Tina took her time getting ready for the meeting. She knew the mustard suit was dated but it made her feel more confident than jeans and a jumper plus the cut of it didn't show how unhealthily skinny she'd become – showing evidence of her illness would show weakness.

"What do you think, Wayne?"

He turned his head from the horseracing on TV. "Clown cheeks could do with toning down a bit."

Tina rushed to the bathroom mirror. He was right, in an effort to portray a picture of hearty healthiness she'd been too heavy-handed with the blusher. She attempted to brush some off and tone it down. Then she set off to the town centre coffee shop.

***

Suzanne started a routine of always walking past the college on her way home from school. It was out of her way but no one was any the wiser because she still got back before her mum was home from work. They never pre-arranged it but Dean was always there, sitting on the wall, waiting for her. If one of them had money they went down the road to MacDonald's otherwise they found a bench somewhere. On their third meeting Dean had kissed her for the first time. It had been scary but exciting. He smelled and tasted of smoke which wasn't too great but she could put up with that because of the way it felt when he touched her. She worried that she was becoming addicted to the thrill of him. She was also worried about him discovering her spare tyre. More than once she'd had to stop his hand finding its way inside the bottom of the loose tops that she favoured. Straight after that first meeting she'd put herself on a diet and started doing sit-ups in her room but so far there didn't seem to have been any change in her shape.

Today they were sharing a Big Mac and a coke between them.

"My dad's getting married in three weeks." She spoke as casually as she could so that it would seem that none of what she had to say was a big deal.

"Oh, yeah." He was taking bigger bites of the burger than she was.

"I can bring a friend to the evening do. So, if you want a free buffet, let me know." As soon as the words were out she picked up the coke and sucked on the straw, pretending she didn't care what he said in reply.

"Yeah, I'll come. As long as I don't need to dress posh?"

The surprise made her swallow the fizzy drink the wrong way and she had a coughing fit. She hadn't expected him to agree so readily. He did like her! She wasn't imagining it. He would get to see her in her glamourous model frock. He would see how beautiful she could be. Perhaps then he'd ask her out properly and people would know they were an item. For now she'd tell her dad and Olivia that they were just friends. She was so happy she let him finish the rest of the burger – it would spoil her diet anyway.

He wiped his mouth with the back of his sleeve. "So are you doing this university nonsense like everyone else or what?"

"That was the plan."

"Not much of a plan to get all that debt and no job at the end of it. And." He stopped and drained the last of the coke. "While you're away things will change. People will change. Nothing will be the same when you come back. We all move on. Three years is a long time."

"What are you saying?" She'd already guessed but asking the question gave her more time. He'd just thrown all her plans up in the air and she wasn't sure how they'd land.

"I'm saying I don't wait for people. I don't wait if they're stuck inside revising or if they've gone away to a waste-of-money university. My life is for living, not waiting."

6

Simon was already in the coffee shop when Olivia arrived. There was no drink in front of him. "I thought we'd order when all three of us were here."

Olivia nodded. She didn't have time for this meeting with some unknown old friend of Simon's mother. There was too much else going on in her head at the moment – the wedding, the plague of nightmares and the fear she was being stalked by a woman in a mustard suit. She'd come because Audrey had gone beyond the call of duty for her all those years ago and she still felt she owed the dead woman something in return. She glanced at her watch. "What's this all about? Who is this woman?"

"All I know is she was in prison with Mum."

"That's her! That's my stalker." Olivia jumped up, unable to take her eyes off the woman in the mustard suit who was pushing open the coffee shop door. Olivia's knuckles went white as she gripped the edge of the table. "She's followed me home from work – at least twice. And now she's followed me here. Mark won't believe me but I swear she's stalking me."

"What do you—" Simon stopped speaking as the woman in the mustard suit let the door swing closed behind her and approached their table.

"Olivia? Simon?"

Simon nodded. "Tina?"

A rush of confusion and fear engulfed Olivia. Her brain struggled to put together the facts. Tina offered her hand to both of them. It was cool and dry despite the warm weather. Why had this woman, who Audrey had known in prison, followed her? Olivia didn't have the courage to ask the question out loud and the woman made no sign of recognition nor mention of their paths having crossed before.

Simon went up to the servery to get their drinks.

"I understand you're getting married soon," Tina said.

"Yes." How far into her life had this woman pried? "There's still a hundred and one things to do, so I can't stop here long today."

"What I have to say won't take long."

Lost for any other conversation they both looked towards the queue at the servery. There were several people in front of Simon. Olivia glanced sideways at Tina. She was drumming the table with the thumb of her right hand and staring at the far wall. Her lips were moving slightly as though she was silently rehearsing a speech. It took only a minute for the rhythmic beat of thumb nail on the plastic-topped table to become annoying. Olivia closed her eyes. It was impossible to close her ears. The tedious tap, tap, tap reminded her of another time and another place. In a reflex action she placed a hand over her stomach. It was the same protective gesture she'd used on that other occasion when this noise had set her on edge. Now she remembered when she'd met her stalker before.

Olivia had been three months pregnant. It was a honeymoon baby and she and Simon were visiting Audrey in prison to give her the good news. Simon always insisted they arrive early at the jail so as not to miss a minute of their allotted time with his mother. They sat on hard plastic chairs waiting to be taken into the visiting area. For some reason she couldn't remember, there'd been a delay and the woman sat nearest to

Olivia had started tapping on a small table that stood between their two chairs. She'd tapped with her right thumb rather than her fingers. Olivia suffered badly with nausea throughout her pregnancy and the drumming noise brought on the familiar warning signs of sickness.

"Please would you stop that?" Olivia had said, indicating the woman's drumming thumb. "I'm pregnant and the least little thing can bring on sickness."

The woman had apologised and stopped immediately. Then she stretched out her arm towards Olivia's belly. "Is it OK if I touch?" Without waiting for a reply she placed her hand on Olivia's still almost flat stomach and ran her fingers over the slight mound beneath the stretchy leggings. She smiled.

Olivia wanted to tell her to take her hand away but the words wouldn't come. She was frozen to the spot like a scared rabbit caught in headlights. Her physical space had been invaded by a stranger and she didn't like it.

"It's for good luck," Tina explained. "My ancestors were gypsies and by stroking a pregnant woman they could pass on either a blessing or a curse to the baby. It also takes away the sickness. You'll not feel ill again during this pregnancy."

With a great effort, Olivia made her muscles work again. She pushed Tina's hand away and stood up. "Don't you dare curse my baby!"

The other people in the waiting room had stared and Simon had tried to calm the situation but Olivia didn't care, she was as mad as hell at the woman's audacity. To this day she was sure the woman had cursed her baby rather than blessed it.

Tina had laughed. "Don't worry. The curse needs some special mumbo jumbo whispering. The right words for it have been lost in the mists of time. But that gentle touch I made will bless the baby."

By now Olivia had been standing behind Simon and clutching at his arm.

"Don't be silly, Liv," said Simon, pulling himself free of his wife and indicating that she should sit back down. "The lady's only trying to be nice."

Olivia knew she was acting childishly but she insisted on swapping seats with Simon to increase the distance between this 'gypsy' and her baby. Then she made a point of looking the other way whilst Simon made polite conversation. She knew he was trying to make up for her rudeness. She stroked her stomach and tried to give good vibes to the baby.

"That's my mum!" Simon's exclamation had made her tune back into the prison waiting-room conversation.

The woman was explaining that she was Tina, Audrey's ex-cellmate and that it felt very odd being back at the prison as a visitor rather than an inmate. "We were best mates for almost four years and I come back occasionally to show Audrey that freedom hasn't made me forget all about her."

Then Simon had started pumping Tina for information about his mother but Olivia had turned her back in an effort to keep her womb protected.

The current drumming on the plastic coffee shop table suddenly stopped. Simon balanced a tray half-on and half-off the table and placed three tall latte glasses plus a handful of sugar sachets and extra-long spoons between Tina and Olivia.

"The three of us did meet once before," Tina said. "It must be nearly thirty years ago."

Simon nodded as he stirred the contents of a second sugar sachet into his coffee. "I remember."

"You cursed my baby." Olivia couldn't stop the accusation.

Tina had the decency to look shocked and Simon frowned.

"You promised the sickness would stop – and it did. But David only lived two months."

Simon leaned across the table and put his hand on Olivia's. "It was a cot death, Liv. Nobody can curse a baby in that way."

Olivia felt the tears welling. She remembered sitting in her nursing chair rocking her dead baby. Her breasts had tingled with the milk ready to feed her son. At the hospital they'd been ushered into a private room and given endless cups of unwanted tea. It had been the worst time of her life. She might have bounced back if she hadn't already been carrying a bucketful of guilt about Audrey. By the time of baby David's funeral she'd been at the bottom of a deep dark pit. Her depression had been the trigger for her divorce from Simon. It had taken her years to forgive herself for the events of the past and to start to respect herself as a person. Only recently had she taken the last step into the sunshine but now Tina was re-triggering all those bad memories and the pit of despair was yawning open again.

"I'm really sorry about your baby. But I swear I didn't cause it. I'm not a witch." Tina was matter of fact and seemed to think that was the subject closed. She pulled an envelope from her handbag and placed it on the table. "I was sorting stuff out the other day and came across this. Your mum gave it to me just before I was released but I forgot all about it. Maybe I shouldn't have opened it. But I did."

Olivia watched Simon's face go pale at the sight of the handwriting on the envelope. His hand shook slightly as he took out the letter and read it. His face gave away nothing of the letter's contents. He passed the single sheet of paper to Olivia. She read the words of the long dead woman and tried to shut down the reaction beginning within the pit of her stomach. She'd seen this handwriting before in a letter she'd torn up and flushed down the toilet almost immediately after receiving it. All the nightmares from her past were rearing up and going for her jugular.

"Can I keep it?" Simon asked. "I don't have much of hers."

"I'd rather you didn't." Tina put the letter back into the envelope and then into her bag. "I wanted to meet you both together because in the letter Audrey promises that you'll help me. And I need help. I need £1000 per month."

"What! That's ridiculous." Simon pushed his chair away from the table, as if getting ready to leave.

"No, wait. This money isn't for me. I've got terminal cancer but I promised my mother on her deathbed, that I'd always make sure my kid brother, Wayne, was looked after. Your mother mentions him in that letter. He's... not the full shilling. He can't earn for himself. The money is for him when I'm gone."

"I'm not going to fall for such a cock and bull story. Please don't contact either of us again."

"Without me your mum would've struggled a lot more than she did in prison. Her life would've been hell. I put my own reputation on the line to help her. You know she killed herself not long after that visit – without me she couldn't survive. She wrote that letter because she knew I deserved your help after what I'd done for her."

"That is not the sort of help my mum would've envisaged. You're abusing the friendship she offered you. Friendship is a two-way street." Simon stood up.

Everyone in the café was staring. Olivia pulled at his hand to make him sit down. He shook her off.

"Compromise," said Tina, a hint of panic and desperation in her voice. "I'll settle for £500 per month."

"Absolutely not." Simon walked out of the café. "You'll get no money from me."

Olivia wanted to go after him but found she couldn't move. Her brain couldn't handle the reawakened grief for her dead baby son, the guilt she carried about Audrey's ultimate sacrifice and, on top of all that, the coordination needed to send a message to her legs to make them stand up and walk.

"You think I've got black magic powers – so a curse on both your houses!" Tina fired the words like bullets and they shot straight to Olivia's core. "You pass that message on to your ungrateful ex-husband."

Tina had been gone for fifteen minutes before Olivia felt strong enough to leave the coffee shop.

7

There was a bench a little way along from the café. Tina sat down and closed her eyes. The confrontation had drained her. She wasn't used to making demands of people. She'd done it clumsily. After the fact she realised she should have appealed more to Simon's loyalty to his mother. She could've given specific examples of how she'd helped Audrey in prison. None came to mind immediately but she could've made stuff up. She could've described the bullying carried out by the other inmates and how they took any small treat that Audrey might have. Sometimes they'd even taken Simon's letters to his mother. But Tina had put a stop to all that and done it at the risk of turning herself into a social pariah. Surely that deserved some reward? But it was too late to go down that avenue now. She'd burned her boats. The only option left was proper blackmail using that piece of creative writing that Audrey had accidentally slipped into the envelope with the letter.

She'd demanded cash because it was the easiest thing to ask for and Tina knew, left to his own devices, Wayne wouldn't be able to budget and keep his spending within the amount of state benefits he received. But cash wasn't the best thing for Wayne. Unless he quit his gang of gambling buddies, any amount of money would slip through his fingers like melted butter. A job would be better than cash – that would limit the amount of free time he had available for losing his wages. But because of his psychological problems and the obsessive rituals he felt compelled to cling to, Wayne's employment history was dire. He'd walked out of jobs that entailed him getting his hands dirty and had been asked to leave other places when he was slow on the uptake or couldn't keep up with the pace of work. A boss would need a big reason to keep Wayne on. Via a circuitous route, using blackmail, Tina might be able to provide Simon with that reason. However, ultimately, Wayne needed someone to replace herself, someone who would look out for him and minimise the financial trouble he could get into. He needed a wife.

Tina leaned forward and pressed the middle three fingers of her left hand against her forehead, giving herself a mini temple massage. The headaches were getting worse. She didn't know whether it was the stress of her situation or whether, unbeknown to the doctors, the cancer was spreading. Sometimes she couldn't think clearly or make decisions. Once she'd stood in the breakfast cereal aisle for a full five minutes, confused by the colours, packaging, shapes and product names that were all so similar. In the end she'd had to weigh up the choices logically and make her eyes move slowly along each shelf until she recognised the only brand that Wayne would eat. If she bought the wrong brand he would eat nothing until the right box had been purchased.

Tina opened her eyes and glanced around, wondering if she had enough energy to walk to the bus stop. As she watched, the door of the coffee shop opened and Olivia walked out. She was blowing her nose. Tina didn't stop to think. This was her chance to win round two of the battle. She went over to Olivia.

"I'm sorry about in there." Tina pointed through the plate glass window of the café. "I went at things a bit cack-handed without thinking it through. It was stupid of me to imagine that

Simon would just pay out money willy-nilly. Have you got a minute so I can explain?"

"Not really. I don't feel too good." Olivia was pale and looked as though she'd been crying.

Tina found it strangely satisfying to see Olivia's confident career woman aura in tatters. Knowing that she had been the one to strip it away gave her the confidence to pursue her goal further. Like a lion sensing the easy prey of an injured animal, she pressed home her advantage. "There's a bench here. Sit down for a minute and you'll feel better."

"I'd rather not."

Tina ignored the feeble protest and linked arms with Olivia to guide her to the bench. "There was another piece of paper in the envelope with that letter from Audrey." Tina spoke as though she and Olivia were best friends. "I didn't bring it with me because it's worth rather a lot of money. In fact, to you, I think it would be priceless."

The two women sat down. Olivia looked confused.

"In the wrong hands that piece of paper would cost you your freedom. You might want to think again about turning down the chance to help me and Wayne."

"I don't know what you're talking about." Olivia stood up.

Tina grabbed her hand. "If you leave now, I'll have no option but to take that piece of paper to the police. That piece of paper is an account, in Audrey's own handwriting and signed and dated by her, of what really happened the night her husband was murdered. Audrey didn't do it but we both know who did."

***

Olivia's legs wobbled and she sat back down on the bench. Despite the warm weather she'd gone icy cold. The worst of her night terrors were turning into reality. Visions of the blood from thirty-odd years ago passed before her. Back then the sticky scarlet stains had spread between the three of them at speed, making them all look equally culpable. But Audrey had confessed as soon as the police arrived and, thanks to the woman's quick thinking, all the other evidence and the only possible motive pointed that way too. Audrey had wiped the knife clean of all prints other than her own and the detectives hadn't dug too deeply, preferring to take things at face value and give themselves an easy life and a certain conviction.

Olivia leaned forwards and put her head in her hands. Then she bent over completely and let her head hang between her knees. She felt sick and light-headed. If she stood or even sat up, she would pass out. The tarmac beneath the bench was spotted with baked on grey splodges of chewing gum and scattered with cigarette butts. A dog had recently defecated beneath the far end of the bench. Olivia couldn't stomach the smell and sat up again quickly before she retched. For a second her head spun and then the earth gradually resettled on its axis. She gripped the edge of the bench.

"It was you. Olivia, you murdered Audrey's husband and let her carry the can for it. Indirectly you murdered her too, she would never have committed suicide if she hadn't been locked up."

Olivia's brain swam. Until now no one had ever accused her of the murder. No one had even hinted that she might be the guilty one. Even, Simon, arriving down the stairs seconds after it happened, had immediately assumed his mother had finally snapped under the strain. Why had Audrey written down what happened after asking Olivia to keep quiet?

"I didn't..." She had to deny it. She mustn't give Tina an inch, or she'd take a mile. But Olivia had never been much of a liar. If the police had pushed for more details when taking her statement she would've caved in and confessed.

"Don't even try to pretend it wasn't you. I have it in black and white that you plunged the knife in."

"I was going to own up." It was impossible to lie when this woman was throwing the truth in her face. "I wanted to go and see her when she was on remand. But I was only sixteen. I didn't know how to organise it. I thought I'd need an adult with me, or an adult's permission – and how was I going to get that without admitting what I'd done? I couldn't even talk to Simon about it honestly."

"Simon still thinks his mother killed his father?"

Olivia nodded.

"How could you let him believe such a terrible thing?"

Olivia closed her eyes. Everything after the stabbing had happened without her doing anything. She had wrestled with the morality of what she let happen so many times. She had thought this torment was behind her but now Tina was ripping open old wounds with no thought for the mental pain it caused. The weeks immediately following the murder had been dark, dark days. Olivia had hardly slept. The murder and its consequences had swirled around her head like some boiling, poisonous liquid in a cauldron, spitting and scalding at will. Olivia's mother was worried by the dark shadows under her eyes, the way she picked at her meals and her refusal to leave the house except under force to go to school. Then the letter from Audrey arrived. Olivia had picked it off the mat after school and before her mum got home from work. She felt a spark of excitement at an envelope with her name on it – she never got letters. But as soon as she glimpsed the content she raced upstairs to her bedroom and shut the door. No one else must ever see this letter.

Dear Olivia,

I hope to be out of here soon. My solicitor is hopeful that it will be seen as self-defence and therefore the judge will be lenient.

I don't regret what you did. Frank had it coming to

him. Life will be better for both Simon and me without him.

Please remain silent about your part in this. If the police think you did it, I suspect that you will be treated much more severely than me, the battered wife. And I may still face a possible jail sentence for perverting the course of justice.

I am forever grateful to you. Please look after Simon for me and do NOT tell him the truth – the fewer people who know about this, the better. Knowing you two are together in a steady relationship makes everything so much easier to bear.

Please destroy this letter.
Yours,
Audrey.

Olivia had read the short note over and over. Audrey was making the decisions for her. Olivia must keep quiet and stick with Simon – then everything would be alright again. Then there was the sound of her mum's key in the lock and the usual call up the stairs.

"I'm home!"

"Upstairs. Won't be a minute."

Olivia had to destroy the letter immediately. It would be found in the wastepaper basket. She had no matches to burn it. In a TV program they'd probably eat it but the thought of swallowing paper made Olivia gag. Instead she locked herself in the bathroom, read Audrey's words one more time and then tore the single page and its envelope into tiny pieces. She watched them fall, confetti-like into the toilet bowl and darken in colour as the water took them. After making sure none of them had gone AWOL on the carpet, Olivia pressed on the flush. She watched as the waterfall took the incriminating sentences away for ever. Then she had gone downstairs with a fake smile and asked about her mum's day.

"Even when you got married you didn't tell him that his mother was innocent?" Tina asked.

Olivia shook her head. "Audrey and I were the only people that ever knew. And now you do too. The guilt was, and is, huge. At least I did what Audrey wanted, so she had less to worry about in prison. I stood by Simon and we got married. We did it on an impulse in Las Vegas. We were only twenty-one and it was an exciting thing to do. Then I got pregnant and then Audrey committed suicide. We were both devastated but I couldn't tell my husband the truth about my feelings. Then David was born. For a while there was brightness and then he died too. All the light had gone from our lives. We were a toxic pair and the only option was separation."

"But things haven't turned out badly for you." The venom in Tina's voice made Olivia flinch. "Nice house, good job, money, car, a very eligible fiancé about to walk you down the aisle. That's far more than Wayne will ever have."

"I always worked hard." Olivia felt wrong-footed. Why should she feel the need to justify her lifestyle? "Throughout my years of depression, work was the only solid thing I had to cling to. Yes, I am extremely lucky to have found Mark – we are good together. But it's too late for us to be blessed with our own children."

"Don't you think it's time to repay more of that huge debt that you owe Audrey?"

Olivia tried to catch up with Tina's inferred meaning. This was a surreal conversation, sitting on a bench on the edge of a shopping centre where businesses were closing up for the day, teenagers were wandering past clutching fast food and workers were hurrying home. To one side the main road was visible and white vans, cars and the occasional bus were taking their passengers about their usual business, oblivious to the drama playing out just yards away from them.

"Audrey promised that you and Simon would always help Wayne and me. You've seen the letter." Tina spoke slowly as though explaining to someone who had difficulty understanding. "It's time for you to keep that promise. It's what Audrey would've wanted. Five hundred pounds a month, that's all I'm asking for, to help secure Wayne's future. It's a small price to pay to get yourself a completely clear conscience. Mark must earn more than enough to keep the pair of you. If you wanted you could give Wayne your whole salary."

"I can't. Not without Mark knowing." Olivia would've willingly put herself on the poverty line to pay off Tina. She wanted this woman and all the bad memories out of her life. But it just wasn't possible. "We're pooling all our finances. We've been taking advice so we can retire early. And Mark must never know what I did – that would be the end of us. I can't give you money because then he'd need to know everything. And if he knows everything there'll be no wedding. I'll have no future."

"But you could do something else?"

Olivia looked at Tina. She had the expression of a deranged woman who'd just had a great idea. Her eyes were too bright and her lips were twisted into a half-smile/half-sneer. Olivia's stomach tightened.

"Simon has the means but no motivation to help someone worse off than himself. He wasn't involved in the killing so I have nothing to use against him, other than to appeal to his conscience to keep his mother's promise. He won't listen to his conscience so he needs to be made afraid. Afraid of me. You are going to make Simon afraid of me."

Olivia clenched her fists and fidgeted on the wooden seat. She could walk briskly away from this menacing voice. Tina didn't seem well enough to be able to catch up with her. But Tina held all the aces and could bring Olivia's life tumbling down like a house of cards. Best to find out what the woman wanted and then try to negotiate her way out of it.

"Perhaps a monetary handout was the wrong thing to ask for. Today's government is all about getting people into work. If Wayne had a job he'd be self-sufficient. I'm going to ask Simon to give Wayne a job at the estate agents."

Olivia let out a breath. That wasn't too bad. Simon could deal with that. He could easily say no because Tina had nothing to use as blackmail against Simon.

"If he refuses," Tina's thin lips smiled at Olivia, "I'll be in touch with you to frighten the pants off him. To make him very afraid of what might happen next." Then she stood up awkwardly, as though in pain, using her arm on the back of the bench as a lever.

Olivia watched her walk slowly back towards the main shopping area. She felt as though she'd been plunged into a limbo of impending doom, without being exactly sure of what she was scared.

8

Loughborough was the last of the university open days on Suzanne's list. It was a Monday and her mum couldn't get the time off work but Olivia and her dad had jumped at the chance of a day out. Her dad was driving. Olivia was talking to him about possible evening buffet menus and he was grunting tetchily in appropriate places. He'd been irritable at breakfast as well. Just before Suzanne had walked into the kitchen she'd heard them talking.

"I'm shattered, Olivia. I can't get by on four hours of sleep. Twice in one night again. It's not on. Let me go with you to the GP and see if he can refer you on anywhere."

"No. The nightmares stopped on their own when I was young. They'll stop again – soon. When the wedding's over, they'll stop. It's just the stress of organising everything. If they don't stop then, I'll go for counselling. It's less than two weeks before we get married – that's not long to wait."

Suzanne's dad had made a big sighing noise as though he didn't believe Olivia, and was only giving into her because he had no ammunition to fight with.

Olivia must have caught his meaning as well. "I'll move into the spare room, tonight. Then your sleep won't be disturbed."

"No! Don't do that."

Suzanne didn't want Olivia to do that either. She had hazy memories of before her parents' divorce. Her mum had started sleeping in the spare room. They tried to hide it from Suzanne but it was obvious that the single bed was being slept in – her mum's books and glasses were on the bedside cabinet. One night Suzanne had been woken by a big row in the hallway about her mum and a mysterious 'him'. It had ended with her mum declaring that she couldn't keep working at their sham of a marriage for the sake of Suzanne. Then the front door had slammed and only her father's footsteps had come up the stairs. Suzanne had started crying. Her dad had come into the bedroom, held her hand and told her that everything was going to be alright.

It wasn't alright. It wasn't alright ever again. Since then Suzanne had spent most week nights with her mum. Initially, the man she'd deduced to be the 'him' from the argument had been there but he disappeared after about a year. After that her mum had never seemed properly happy again. At least every other weekend Suzanne spent with her dad. She preferred being with her dad. He was more laid back. She loved Olivia and wished she could move in with the both of them permanently but that would upset her mum.

In the car Suzanne's eyes were closed and she was pretending to be asleep but her brain was hyperactive. She was worrying a little bit about her dad and Olivia – but not too much because Olivia had looked so radiant in her wedding dress. She and Dad might have disagreements but they wouldn't split up.

She was worrying a little bit about what Olivia and her parents would say when they met Dean on the evening of the wedding. She was sure they'd disapprove. They wouldn't see past the accent. They wouldn't realise how tender and loving he could be and the way he could make you laugh. And laughing was good when you'd been called 'cushion tummy' in the changing-rooms after PE yet again. Not that she'd ever admitted to Dean about that. When she was with Dean she always felt as attractive as she had in the bridal shop.

She was worrying a lot about the whole university thing. It was happening like a tidal wave. She'd allowed herself to be swept along with it because nobody had told her there was an alternative. It was like, if you were clever enough to do A' levels then you automatically went to university afterwards. If you weren't clever enough for A' levels you went to college after GCSEs and learned something practical, like Dean and his mates. Where was the middle ground? Without being big-headed about it, Suzanne knew she was clever and that an Economics degree would be a leg up into a career. But Dean had put doubts into her head and university meant that she would lose him. She knew it was stupid to change her whole future because of a boy but if university really was the place for her, Dean wouldn't have been able to sow those seeds of doubt, would he? Perhaps university wouldn't suit her.

"This place should go to the top of the UCAS list," her dad said.

They were drinking coffee, standing up, from takeaway cups in the Students' Union. All the seats were taken by other teenagers and their parents. Suzanne kept glancing round for a seat, she was tired. They'd had a tour round the department, a tour round some of the halls and sat through talks about finance, course structure and exchange schemes with universities abroad.

"I like it too," Olivia said. "And it's not too far if you want to come home for the odd weekend."

Suzanne moved her weight from one foot to the other and frowned. It was now or never. She had to tell them. They couldn't go on planning her future like this. "I'm not sure university's for me."

There was a sort of silence. Olivia and her dad didn't speak but there was background talking going on all around them.

Her dad looked like he was trying to make sense of something he didn't understand. "But the teachers are predicting you three As. You'll be brilliant."

"I feel like I'm jumping into university without thinking," Suzanne said. "I haven't researched any other options. There might be something more suitable."

"But you're academic. We've always known that. You'd be stupid to throw away the chance of higher education." He sounded exasperated and, from past experience, Suzanne knew that in a minute he'd get full-blown angry.

"Mark," Olivia's voice was gently reprimanding. "Suzanne's right. There's a few months before applications have to be in. Let her explore the options and then make a decision."

Suzanne smiled gratefully at Olivia. Perhaps she might even be understanding when she met Dean.

***

Simon sat down at his desk and opened his briefcase. He'd been out of the office most of the morning showing properties to prospective buyers. He rarely did viewings these days but the branch was short staffed and finding it hard to recruit. Plus he enjoyed getting out at the sharp end every now and again and meeting buyers and vendors. It was the connection with people that he liked. But it meant the rest of the day was a game of catch-up with emails and admin. The receptionist put a pile of post in front of him and asked if he'd like a coffee.

"Yes, please, Rachel – I'm gasping."

A CV for one of the vacant posts was on top of the pile of pre-opened envelopes. The applicant's name was Wayne Mallinson. The passport photo stapled to the application immediately reminded him of Tina. He'd only spent a few minutes with her the other day but he could still visualise every detail of her appearance. Wayne's face was much chubbier but the pair had the same eyes and jaw line. He didn't share his sister's tense, drawn expression, Wayne's face was more open and relaxed.

Simon took a couple of deep breaths. He hadn't been expecting this, at the confrontation in the café he'd thought he'd made it plain that he wanted nothing to do with Tina and her greedy demands.

"Are you alright? You've gone a bit pale." The receptionist put a custard cream next to the mug on his desk.

"I'm fine. It's probably low blood sugar. I didn't have time for breakfast."

Simon skimmed through the CV. It contained nothing that was relevant to working in the residential property sector. There was no reason for Simon to consider employing Wayne. For a second Simon's conscience pricked over the promise his mother had made to Tina in that handwritten letter. His mum had always been concerned about others. He shook it off. That promise had been made in another world three decades ago, his mother couldn't have foreseen what would happen.

"Rachel," he called the receptionist over and handed her the CV. "Please can you send a standard rejection letter to this applicant? First class, please." The sooner Tina and Wayne got the message that he wasn't playing ball, the better.

Joanne called later and asked him to pick up a bottle of wine on his way round to her house for dinner.

"White would be good," she said. "We're having chicken."

Simon put the phone down with a smile. He'd been considering whether to propose to Joanne but was worried it might be too early and she'd run a mile. It was only two years since her husband had died and six months since they'd started seeing each other. Initially Joanne had put up a protective guard when she was out with Simon and he'd struggled to find the real woman underneath.

"She's scared of destroying Roger's memory by having

another man in her life," Olivia had said, when he sought her advice. "You're going to have to go slowly, slowly."

But eventually Joanne's warmth and sense of fun broke through the façade and Simon enjoyed discovering her full personality. He knew she felt the same way when she offered to cook him dinner for the first time. By doing this, she was inviting him into the space she and Roger had created together and called home. It was a major step forward. When he'd arrived she'd been honest with him about how she was coping with this progression of their relationship.

"I don't want any echoes of Roger around to make me feel guilty," she'd said. "I've deliberately chosen recipes that I've never cooked before and I've bought a new set of crockery and wine glasses – the others were wedding gifts. And I've also removed all the photos – tonight is about me and you."

"I really appreciate that," he'd said, taken her in his arms and kissed her.

As the oven timer went off she'd laughed and pulled away. "It does mean you're a guinea pig as I cook my way through unchartered territory."

She'd cooked him many more meals since then and one of her new recipes, a variation on beef wellington, had become their favourite. It probably wasn't that tonight since she'd specified white wine.

"I've made something up," she announced when he walked into the kitchen. "It's to use up the mushrooms and cream that I had left in the fridge. Fingers crossed it turns out OK."

After the meal they drank coffee in the lounge as the last of the summer daylight disappeared.

"I'm having the bedroom decorated next week." Joanne stared at him as though there was a hidden meaning behind her words. "I've chosen new curtains as well but I decided against changing the carpet. Silly to spend all that money just for the sake of it."

"What colour?" Simon thought he was understanding her but he wanted to be absolutely sure before articulating it and scaring her off.

"Light blue walls and darker blue curtains."

Simon had never seen the old décor. "Sounds good. Will I be allowed to admire it when it's done?"

"Absolutely." There was a glint in Joanne's eye. "Roger papered that room and I thought... well, I thought it was time for a new start. And you will be very welcome in there."

Simon pulled her close and wondered whether he should propose sooner or later. Following Joanne's pace had worked well so far, perhaps he'd allow her to continue taking the lead.

9

"Can I help you?" The young woman at the desk facing the door of the estate agency was pretty and smartly dressed.

"I need a word with Simon Frome." Tina gestured towards the back of the office where she could see Simon sitting at a desk. He was deep in conversation with a couple.

"As you can see he's with clients at the moment. Do you have an appointment?" The woman consulted her computer screen.

Tina noticed a nameplate on the desk. "No, Rachel. I don't 'ave an appointment. But I can wait until he's free."

"Perhaps someone else can help you?" Rachel glanced behind her at two other members of staff. "Are you interested in sales or lettings?"

"Neither. It's a personal matter."

Rachel raised her eyebrows. "You better take a seat."

Tina settled herself down and picked up a local paper. She flicked through the pages. The middle section was full of houses and flats at prices she and Wayne could never afford. Even the private rental rates made her eyes water. Perhaps she shouldn't grumble about their council flat and benefits. Of course Wayne would have to come off the benefits when he was settled in working here. No point pushing their luck by trying to have their cake and eat it – too many people got caught these days.

She put the paper down. Rachel caught her eye and then looked quickly away. The girl was obviously dying to know what the personal business was. Tina stared at Simon. He glanced up from his conversation, over the shoulders of the couple sitting in front of him. She gave him a smile. He turned his head quickly but Tina didn't avert her gaze. Whenever he raised his eyes she was there staring at him, intimidating him. He needed to know she meant business. She wasn't going to leave here today without a result.

Finally he was standing up, shaking hands with the couple and ushering them to the door. Rachel pointed to Tina and said something in a low voice to Simon.

"This way, please." He spoke without a smile.

"Would you like coffee?" Rachel followed them.

"No, we won't be—"

"Yes, please, love." Tina smiled at the girl. "I like it white with one sugar."

"What do you want?" Simon said as soon as they were out of earshot of Rachel. His voice was sharp and reinforced Tina's determination to beat him down and get her own way.

"You rejected Wayne's job application. That isn't the way to treat an old friend of your mother's, especially an old friend who helped your mum through her darkest time."

Rachel arrived with the mugs and fussed around with coasters and biscuits. The receptionist couldn't hide the fact that she was trying to overhear what Simon's personal business was.

"Thank you, Rachel," Simon said. "Please can you see to the gentleman who's just walked in?"

Rachel walked slowly back towards the reception area.

"If you can't give Wayne a job then I can't guarantee the safety of your girlfriend, Joanne."

"What?" Simon's face was a lovely mixture of confusion, amazement and fear.

"You heard right what I said."

"Look." Simon placed his hands on the desk and leaned forward slightly. "I'm sorry for Wayne and for you and for the sad situation you find yourselves in but this is a business not a charity. Wayne has no relevant experience. He'll be a deadweight. If I give him a job, my other staff will crucify me because they'll have to carry him."

"It's a good thing I didn't think like that when I met your mum. Befriending 'er didn't do me any favours with the other inmates. Quite often it felt like I was being crucified. But we have to help those less well off than ourselves, otherwise where would the world be? Now, you do your bit for humanity by offering Wayne a job, or be prepared to see your girlfriend hurt. I don't think pretty Joanne deserves that, do you?"

"Are you blackmailing me?"

Tina raised her eyebrows, sat back in her chair and gazed at Simon. He kept swallowing, looking at his desk and fiddling with his pens. She liked the way he shifted uneasily in his chair. This feeling of power was good. It was a shame she'd discovered it so near the end of her life.

Rachel approached again. "More coffee?" she asked brightly.

"No." Simon snapped. "Are the details for that house in Warwick Road complete? I promised the vendor they'd be uploaded to the website today."

Rachel wandered off again.

"So, are you going to put Joanne at risk? She's suffered a lot already with losing her 'usband. A shame if a nice girl like that gets hurt again."

"I'm not giving in to blackmail." There was a slight tremor in his voice. "But we're short-staffed and I'm a fair person so I'll give Wayne a trial. He can start tomorrow. But if he doesn't pull his weight and learn quickly then he's out."

Tina smiled and leaned over the desk to shake Simon's hand. He seemed reluctant to touch her and his grip was weak. Wayne was unlikely to meet Simon's expectations of a competent worker and a quick learner but, once her brother was in here, there'd be no way on earth that Simon could get him out again – Tina would make sure of that.

**

It was a few minutes after nine the next morning when Wayne pushed open the door of the estate agency. The prospect of a 'proper' job terrified him but Tina had insisted he must become self-sufficient to survive after she was gone. Tina didn't understand that being with other people all day would compromise his rituals and then bad things would happen. This was the beginning of the end.

He felt uncomfortable in the new shirt and tie Tina had made him wear. The buttons were tight around his neck and across his paunch.

"The weather's warm so you won't need a jacket," his sister had said, fussing as though he was still a kid. "And don't waste this chance – it would make our mum real proud to know you're working in a proper office. I know it won't be easy for you but just do exactly as you're told."

He looked at his hands. They were red and rough from washing. He'd been so nervous this morning he'd had to wash them forty-nine times instead of the usual seven.

"Can I help you, sir?"

The young receptionist was pretty. Wayne gave her his best smile but she was already glancing back at her computer screen.

"I'm 'ere for the job. I was told to ask for Simon Frome."

"What's your name?"

"Wayne Mallinson." He tried smiling again.

"Come with me, please." She didn't return his grin.

He followed her to the back of the office. Simon was concentrating on a computer screen, a mug of coffee at his elbow.

"Wayne Mallinson to see you, Simon."

"Hello, Wayne. Thanks, Rachel."

"Coffee, Wayne?" Rachel asked.

He wondered whether he could ask for tea with the milk separately, so that he could make sure that exactly the right amount went into the mug.

Before Wayne could speak, Simon shook his head. "I'll show Wayne the kitchen in a minute. Then he'll be able to make his own and contribute to the kitty. First, Wayne, I need you to fill out this new starter form for HR. A photocopy of your passport needs to go with that. Have you got it?"

Whilst Simon went to photocopy the passport, Wayne filled in the rest of the form, copying his bank details from his debit card and his National Insurance number from the bit of paper Tina had put in his pocket that morning. Next Simon gave him a quick tour of the office. Wayne tried not to cringe at the unavoidable skin to skin contact as strangers shook hands with him. In the kitchen Simon waited whilst Wayne took a five pound note from his pocket and stuffed it in the kitty jar.

"Now I suggest you make yourself popular by getting everyone's drink order and brewing up. I'll have a white tea with no sugar. When you're done, go see Rachel. She'll show you how to upload new house details on to the website. We've got a backlog of those to do."

As soon as Simon left him, Wayne washed his hands seven times in the kitchen sink, using washing up liquid in the absence of soap. There was only a thin, damp tea towel for drying, so rather than risk the germs, he gave several good shakes of the wrist and then used the clean handkerchief from his pocket to finish the drying process. He managed to tour the office by himself, write down a list of drinks and make them all. He didn't have his special mug with the painted milk line but he guessed the level as best he could. There was no teapot either, so he slopped the teabags around and tried to ignore the way it grated on his nerves. No one else seemed to mind about the colour of their drink but his was all wrong. He tipped it away, not wanting to encourage the creatures of doom into his life with a drink that was the wrong shade of brown.

Then he sat next to Rachel on a twirly office chair to learn about putting houses on the internet. He watched her fingers race over the keyboard and click continuously on the mouse. She did everything too quickly: click, click, enter a password, check a box, click, click, browse for a photo, click, check a box, click, click, browse for the house details.

"You do the next one." Rachel scooted her wheeled chair to one side of the desk so that Wayne could take her place.

As she turned to answer a phone call, he surreptitiously wiped the mouse clean with the damp handkerchief from his pocket. The domed lump of plastic still felt slightly warm from her touch and he tried not to show his distaste.

Until then Wayne's smartphone was the nearest he'd got to operating a computer. He cautiously started moving the mouse. He got the cursor in the right place and clicked. He forgot what came next. Rachel explained again. He clicked and Rachel gave another instruction. Wayne's head was spinning. If this was a coveted white collar job, he wasn't impressed. His shoulders were beginning to ache from hunching tensely over the screen, his wrist and hand were hurting from clutching the mouse and every time a customer came in he lost the thread of what Rachel was saying because she had to go and help them. Eventually Rachel gave a big sigh, as though she was coming to the end of her patience, and said she'd write out instructions for him so he could try it at his own pace at his own desk.

Without Rachel looking over his shoulder, Wayne relaxed and made progress. He followed the numbered instructions on the piece of paper she'd given him. By lunchtime he'd managed to get his first set of house details loaded up onto the estate agency's website. Rachel was busy with a customer but she indicated that he should take his lunchbreak. He found a quiet place on a bench in the park to perform the ritual with his mother's photo – if he didn't do it there'd be disaster in the afternoon. He took out the creased image. The picture wouldn't last much longer, some of the crease lines were already turning into small tears. Wayne worried that one day it would just disintegrate and then his whole life would fall apart – especially if Tina was gone too. He set the timer on his watch. For exactly seven minutes he looked in silence at the picture of his mum and thought how kind and gentle she'd been. Then he kissed her image seven times and slipped it back in his pocket. For a while he sat and looked at the trees and grass around him and wondered where people went to when they died. Would Tina go and join their mum? If so, he'd like to go too. When he went back an hour later, the estate agency was in uproar.

Simon grabbed Wayne's arm and pulled him towards the back of the shop. "Your trial here is terminated," he hissed. "Jokers are not welcome."

"I'm not a joker." Wayne tried to shake himself free. Simon's nails were digging painfully into his fleshy upper arm. "I've done exactly what I was told."

"So why did you lose a zero off the price of that house you uploaded? Instead of 'offers in the region of £500,000', you put 'offers in the region of £50,000'. The phone's never stopped ringing. The vendor is fuming and he's on his way here now. He's threatening to move his business to one of our competitors."

Wayne felt his cheeks flame with shame. He swallowed and blinked hard. In his mind he could see the disappointed faces of Tina and his mother. They were expressions he'd seen often but he'd so wanted to make them proud for once.

"Get your things and leave." Simon released his grip.

Wherever his mother was, she'd know that he'd messed up this chance of a proper job. Tina's sad face would have to be faced in the flesh. She always tried so hard to help him and every time he failed. Wayne didn't say anything, fearful his voice would shake and he might even cry. He touched the photo in his pocket. He put his shoulders back and walked out of the estate agency without looking anyone in the eye. Before the door closed behind him, he heard Simon berating Rachel for leaving Wayne unsupervised. It wasn't Rachel's fault. It was his own fault for being so thick.

***

Olivia took several deep breaths after the call ended. Mark was in the kitchen, it was his turn to cook, and he hadn't overheard Tina giving her abhorrent orders. Olivia clenched and unclenched her fists and tried to get a grip on her options. According to Tina, there were three. Olivia could do nothing and wait for the police to come knocking after Tina showed them Audrey's written account of the night of the murder. She could pay £500 per month to Wayne for the rest of his life. Or she could carry out the blackmail threat Tina had made to Simon and thus force him into reinstate Wayne at the estate agency. Specifically, Tina wanted Olivia to put doubts into Joanne's head about her relationship with Simon *and* give her a physical fright as well – so that Simon would fear both for the future of their relationship and for Joanne's personal safety. Olivia realised Tina must have been watching them all closely and for some time to realise how deeply Simon cared for Joanne. He would do anything to protect her and their relationship – and that would include capitulating to Tina's blackmail.

Tina's call hadn't come totally out of the blue. Simon had phoned earlier and told Olivia about Wayne's catastrophic mistake and how Tina had ranted down the phone at him about her brother losing his job. Apparently she'd finished by saying, 'You and that beloved girlfriend of yours will pay for this'.

Simon said he wasn't worried, Tina didn't have the strength to hurt a fly and Wayne didn't have the guts or the sense. Olivia had remained silent but her stomach had turned over at Simon's words – she knew Tina would ask *her* to convert the words into deeds.

The first of the three options was never going to happen. She couldn't risk being locked up forever. The thought of prison terrified her – she didn't have Audrey's courage. The third option meant she would lose her best female friend and her best male friend. They would never forgive her for turning traitor and carrying out Tina's threats. Despite the problems that had led to their divorce, she valued the relationship she still had with Simon. Their shared experience of horrific trauma in their teenage years had created a bond that lasted forever – or until one of them turned on the other, as she was being asked to do. Losing these two friends and seeing them hurt through her actions as a conduit of blackmail would be unbearable. But the prospect of jail was worse. Option two, paying the money, would solve everything but required the ability to produce a large amount of money every month forever – without the knowledge of her new husband.

The kitchen smelt of tomato sauce with the faint twang of garlic. Mark was cooking spaghetti Bolognese.

"After we're married," he said, "will I have a proper wife who does all the cooking, instead of this taking it in turns business?"

For a second Olivia thought he was being serious and then his face broke into a grin and he gave her a playful pat on the bottom. "Just joking!"

"Actually, I wanted to talk about after we're married," she said cautiously. "I know we agreed that the best thing was to be totally transparent about what money was coming in and going out so we could plan an early retirement. But I wondered if we could still retain some of our financial privacy?"

"It's a bit late for that. We went through all the figures with the financial advisor. We each know what capital the other has, how much they earn and roughly how it gets spent, give or take the odd haircut or new pair of shoes. Or several new pairs of shoes in your case!"

It was Olivia's turn to give Mark the expected playful slap, even though she wanted him to take this discussion seriously.

He pretended to be hurt. "OK, OK, I give in. We'll double your shoe allowance if you promise not to be a husband-beater."

"But all this transparency means we don't have any privacy. What if I want a girly weekend away in Paris with Joanne?"

"That's fine. The purpose of this is not to stop you enjoying yourself. It's to help with budgeting and saving. We need to know about any large expenditure or new regular payments that either of us might have, not to necessarily stop it but so we can allow for it in our planning. For instance, I'm likely to have to make regular payments to help fund Suzanne through university."

"Yes, I'm perfectly fine with that, if she decides to go. But what if I wanted to make similar payments?"

"To Suzanne? No, not a good idea. We don't want to make life too easy for her – she's got to understand the concept of working for her money. A kind thought though." Mark turned to the hob and gave the Bolognese sauce a stir. Then he blew on the end of the wooden spoon and tasted it, making a murmur of appreciation.

"No, not to Suzanne. To someone else."

"Who?"

"There, you see, this arrangement means that we have no privacy to do what we want with our money."

"Who do you want to pay money to?" Mark had put the spoon down and was looking at her with a frown on his face.

"No one. It was a hypothetical question."

Mark took a step towards her and put his hands on her shoulders. He gave a gentle squeeze. "I don't want to repeat the mistakes I made with Suzanne's mum. That's why I won't let you move into the spare room. Admittedly, money was scarcer back then but she bought on credit through a catalogue and I went into debt on a credit card. Before we knew it everything blew up in our faces and we couldn't meet the mortgage payments. Then she fell into the arms of someone better off than me. It didn't last, but that's another story. If you want to spend money, and we can afford it, that's fine but tell me first. I don't need to know to the nearest lipstick or Starbucks latte."

Olivia sighed. "Forget I ever said anything. That looks nearly ready, shouldn't the spaghetti be going in to boil now?"

"Too many cooks." Mark pointed to the kitchen door. "Shoo!"

Olivia agreed with Mark's money philosophy. As a married couple they would operate as a single unit and therefore transparency was essential. And even if she did find a way of secretly setting up a £500 monthly payment, she wouldn't be able to finance that sort of sum for ever, certainly not once she retired. She had no alternative but to go for option three. Tina had demanded she act tomorrow. With the threat of her evil secret being exposed to the police, Olivia didn't dare disobey. She texted Joanne to arrange to meet her for a drink the following evening.

Later, Suzanne arrived at the house. She rang the doorbell once, then used her key and shouted a greeting. Olivia followed Mark into the hall to see her.

"I can't stop. Mum's waiting outside but I need to ask you both something." Suzanne was hovering awkwardly by the front door.

"If it's about university, I still think you should go. What does your mother think?"

"Don't jump to conclusions, Mark. Let's hear Suzanne's question first."

Suzanne cast Olivia a grateful glance. "You said I could bring a friend to the evening do. Is it OK if it's a boy?"

Olivia looked at Mark. Suzanne was his daughter so this wasn't her call but she crossed her fingers that he'd say yes. He was already building barriers between himself and Suzanne over the university business. Please don't let him do it over this as well, she thought.

"A boy? You mean a boyfriend?"

"Not exactly, officially. But sort of." Suzanne looked embarrassed and her face was going scarlet.

"I don't think so. Not someone we don't know. Bring one of your girlfriends, one we've met before. A wedding isn't the place for strangers."

Olivia wanted to thump him.

Suzanne looked at the floor, burrowing the toe of her shoe into the carpet. "What if I've already asked him?" Her voice was a mumble.

"Then you'll have to un-ask him."

A car horn sounded outside. "Mum's in a hurry." She scuttled out of the door without looking either of them in the eye.

"That was not the right answer," said Olivia.

"She's my daughter."

10

Olivia and Joanne were sipping wine in a bar across the canal from the International Convention Centre.

"Are things getting serious between you and Simon?" Olivia ventured. "You're walking about on cloud nine the whole time now."

"If he asked me to marry him, I'd say yes immediately."

"Wow!" Olivia sat back in her chair. This wasn't good. Could she wreck her best friend's happiness to secure her own future? "That's what I call serious. So have you gone through the bedroom door yet?"

"It's imminent. Guilt over Roger was holding me back but slowly I'm getting past that. I've discovered the trick is to change things around at home so I don't appear to be betraying Roger by doing with Simon exactly what I did with Roger. Just using new crockery or buying different wine is enough. I'm hoping that re-decorating the bedroom will work. If it doesn't I'll move into the spare room. Or maybe we'll go to a hotel." The mischievous glint in her friend's eye tore at Olivia's core.

"And he's been happy to wait?"

"Absolutely, he's the perfect gentleman. He doesn't talk much about his past but I get the impression that, since you, he's had only one serious relationship and that ended badly. I think he licked his wounds for a long time. Maybe that helps him appreciate where I'm coming from."

"I don't want you to get hurt, Joanne." Olivia scraped her chair closer to the round wooden table to allow someone to squeeze past behind her. "Losing Roger was bad enough and now you're just starting to live again. Don't get in too deep until you're sure he feels the same way. For example, are you certain you're the only one he's seeing at the moment?"

"Of course I am." The words were firm but Joanne's forehead creased.

"I wasn't going to say anything because I thought your relationship was only casual." Olivia felt as though she was turning the screw on an instrument of torture. Despite the pain, there could be no stopping now, Simon had to be frightened into doing Tina's bidding and that meant hurting his girlfriend. "If you're serious, you need to know something."

"Need to know what?" A flash of fear crossed Joanne's face.

A man in jeans and a leather jacket asked if he could remove one of the unused chairs from their table. Olivia rescued her handbag from its seat and nestled it securely between her feet under the table.

"Need to know what?" Joanne repeated, her voice going up a notch in volume.

"I thought I saw him out with someone else." She spoke quietly, hating herself for the barbed lie. "A blonde woman, younger than us and with a figure to die for."

"You think he's two-timing me?" Joanne's eyes widened. "We've been seeing each other nearly every day. He's had no time to get involved with anyone else."

"You'd be surprised where men find the time for these things. Someone at work, her husband kept up a double life for years before she became suspicious."

"Stop it!" Joanne put her hands over her ears. "I don't believe you. Maybe Simon was like that when you were married to him but he's not like that with me."

The reference to her failed marriage felt like a punch below the belt to Olivia. Then she remembered she was making up the stories, not Joanne. She needed to say sufficient to put her friends' relationship on the rocks but little enough to allow it to be saved by Simon – as long as Tina's blackmail demand of a job reinstatement at the estate agents for Wayne was met. "You've been through enough, Joanne, and you don't deserve to be hurt. Tread carefully, that's all I'm saying. Roger's life insurance left you comfortably off. Maybe Simon's a gold digger. When we married I'd just inherited a house from my parents – perhaps he was after my money." Olivia knew this was not true – Simon had asked for nothing when they got divorced but it made her allegations more plausible.

"I need some fresh air." Joanne stood up and pulled on her jacket.

"I've upset you. I'm sorry – you know me, I'm always a glass half empty person. Perhaps I'm wrong. Perhaps this blonde was a work colleague or a neighbour or something." Olivia hadn't expected it to be so easy to make Joanne believe her. Now her friend's eyes were bright, her cheeks flushed and she was battling to keep the muscles in the lower part of her mouth in check. In a second she would break down in tears. Olivia wished she could backpedal and make everything alright again.

"I have to go. I feel like I'm suffocating in here." Joanne turned, looking for the exit.

The bar was busy now and the ceiling fan was inadequately stirring the warm fug of conversation and laughter.

"Let me come with you. You shouldn't be wandering around on your own in this state." The lead weight of dread in Olivia's stomach grew as she realised it was time for the second part of her task.

Joanne frowned and then shrugged as if she didn't care

whether or not Olivia followed her. They had to push between tables to get out of the bar and it was just as busy outside. The bars and restaurants around Brindleyplace were a magnet for young professionals who sat outside in the evening sunshine enjoying wine and beer. But Joanne walked as though she were on a mission and Olivia had to trot to keep up. Conveniently her friend strode towards the ICC and then went down the steps to the canal bank and headed away from the buzz of people towards the relative quiet of the canal basin. Olivia wished she hadn't worn heels; her shoes kept catching in the crannies along the towpath. Joanne was wearing flat ballet pumps and was able to keep ahead. Eventually her friend stopped walking and stood at the water's edge staring into its depths.

"I used to think it would be so easy to join Roger. I thought about pills, about slitting my wrists in the bath or jumping from a tower block but I was too cowardly to follow any of them through. Now I wish I had. Until I met Simon every day was a constant battle against loneliness." Joanne looked from the dark water to Olivia. "Then I learned to love again. And now you're telling me my new love can't be trusted. You're saying he's two-timing me with some glamorous young blonde." There was a catch in Joanne's voice as though she was about to cry. "If it's going to be this difficult to find a new companion then I'm not interested. I'm not interested in life anymore." Joanne stared once more into the depths. Her toes were slightly over the edge of the towpath above the water. She swayed and then steadied herself.

Olivia wanted to cry at the terrible impact her words had had on her friend. It had been too easy to lie to Joanne and make her distraught. But the worst was still to be done. Olivia placed a hand on her friend's shoulder. She simply had to give a gentle push. The canal wasn't deep enough for Joanne to drown, that wasn't the purpose of the exercise. The purpose of the exercise was to frighten Simon into thinking Joanne would sustain a worse physical injury if he didn't capitulate to Tina's demands. This evening Olivia had to show Simon that Tina meant business. She *had* to push Joanne because if she didn't, Tina would push Olivia's entire future into oblivion. Audrey's account of the murder would go to the police, Olivia would be arrested, Mark would leave her and she would spend the rest of her days behind bars – perhaps driven to suicide in the same way that Audrey had been.

Joanne was so near the edge she would tip in easily. Olivia's mouth was dry. The hand that wasn't resting on Joanne's shoulder was shaking. She felt slightly sick.

A man with a dog was walking towards them. He was about a hundred yards away. A narrow boat was chugging slowly in the same direction. They were too far away to see whether a jump or a push had propelled Joanne into the water.

"I'm sure you don't mean that, Joanne. You have everything to live for." Olivia spoke more loudly now so that her voice would carry in the still air. To her own ears the words sounded forced and shaky. The man with the dog was getting nearer. If he had good hearing she had to be careful what he overheard. "Think about your two daughters. I know they're grown-up and independent but if you jump now and kill yourself, they will live with the guilt for the rest of their lives."

"I don't want to be a burden to them. They don't want the responsibility of a lonely, ageing mother holding them back."

Olivia tensed the muscles in her arm ready for the push. One split second was all it would take. Joanne and Simon would never forgive her but the wedding and her future with Mark would be secure. She wouldn't lose the man she loved.

Then the conscience she'd banished to a dark corner on leaving the house, started worming its way out into the brightness. She'd fought against its demands at sixteen and had won. It had turned into a hollow victory. It wasn't worth the destruction of more lives for another hollow victory.

She couldn't go through with it. Whatever the cost to her personally she couldn't scare her best friend in this way or let her think she'd been duped by a gold-digging boyfriend. Joanne didn't deserve it and Simon didn't deserve it. But she, Olivia, did deserve a lifetime in prison. She deserved whatever hellish treatment the other prisoners gave her. She deserved to be driven to suicide. She deserved it for what she'd done to Audrey, to Simon's dad and for what she had been so willing to do to her best friend.

"Let's go home, Joanne. I spoke out of turn about Simon. It's obvious to anyone that he's crazy about you. I just wanted to make you think before you committed yourself to him." Olivia pulled Joanne back from the edge and gave her a hug. Joanne was tense and didn't respond to the affection, she stood there like a post.

Olivia wondered if Tina would go to the police immediately she heard her blackmail threat to Simon hadn't been carried out. What would the police do? Would there be any breathing space for her to explain herself to Mark before the handcuffs went on? She thought of the wedding dress that would never now be worn. Would Suzanne still wear her dress to the school prom if it was tainted by an almost-stepmother who turned out to be a murderer?

"Now you're confusing me!" Joanne came to life and shook herself free of Olivia. "Did you see Mark with someone else or not?"

"No. I swear."

The dog was galloping along the canal bank. It was an excited golden Labrador. A tennis ball, thrown by the man, bounced at a weird angle on the stones immediately in front of Joanne and ricocheted into the water. The dog banged against both their legs in his haste to jump in the canal after the ball. Olivia twisted over on her ankle and cursed her spindly heels again.

There was a splash and a scream followed by chaos. Joanne

had been knocked in the water with the dog. Olivia screamed. Then she realised that the narrow boat was only a few yards away and heading directly for her friend. "The boat's going to mow her down," she shouted to anybody that might hear. "Help!"

The man at the boat's tiller was waving and yelling incomprehensibly as he tried to swing the boat away from Joanne's head and shoulders which were on the surface of the water. Her arms were floundering and she was making no progress towards the bank.

The dog man was running along the towpath calling the animal's name. "Nemo! Nemo!"

The dog had retrieved the ball and was back on the bank. Ignoring the man's shouts, he dropped the ball at Olivia's feet, shook himself vigorously and barked expectantly. His tail sprayed droplets of water in its wagging wake. Joanne was waving, splashing and shouting. Olivia felt as though she was starring in a disaster movie. Her heart was about to escape her chest. She was terrified for her friend's safety. The noise of the boat's engine grew louder. Joanne's screams increased in volume and terror. Olivia glanced round for a lifebelt but the nearest post was naked of its precious cargo. There was no choice, she had to go into the water and drag Joanne to safety. She kicked off her high-heels and sat on the edge of the path, her legs dangling, ready to lever herself into the dankness. The chill of the water made her wince. The man on the boat had the handle of the tiller pulled right to one side. Finally it veered across the canal and got nearer to the opposite bank, out of Joanne's way.

"Thank the lord," whispered Olivia and prepared to drop into the water.

"No! I'll go in." The dog man had come up behind her. He removed his jacket, kicked off his shoes and slipped gingerly into the water. He took a couple of steps and then held an arm out to Joanne. "Grab hold and I'll give you a pull."

Gradually he drew her to the shore and then gave her a leg up to climb out. Olivia helped her to her feet. Joanne stood sodden and shivering on the towpath. The man used his arms on the side of the bank to pull himself out. He put his leather jacket around Joanne's shoulders. She was shaking uncontrollably.

"Did you trip?" he asked. "There ought to be railings along this edge."

Joanne shook her head. She seemed unable to speak.

"It was your dog racing after the ball," Olivia answered the man on her friend's behalf. "He crashed into her legs and knocked her in."

"I am so sorry." The man looked aghast and couldn't apologise enough. "I don't know what to say."

"Don't worry. It was an accident." Joanne's voice was weak.

"We need to get you straight home. You better have this back." Olivia handed the leather jacket back to the man and put her own flimsy, linen jacket around her friend. "Let's get back up onto Broad Street and flag a taxi."

Olivia forced her shoes back on her sodden feet. The man did the same. Instead of attempting to tie the soaked laces he pushed them down the inside of each shoe.

The man replaced his jacket on top of Olivia's and followed them up from the canal bank on to the main road. Joanne's shoes were at the bottom of the canal and every step in stockinged-feet made her wince. Olivia kept a protective arm around her friend. The dog was still excited but it was on a tight lead. Olivia glanced backwards and saw the boat was back in the middle of the canal and moving off. The man at the tiller gave her a wave.

"Keep my jacket for now, love," said the man. "Give me your address and I'll call round for it later. Otherwise you'll catch pneumonia."

"Thank you," Joanne said, with a pathetically grateful look on her face.

"But you're just as wet as she is. You take the jacket," said

Olivia, gently removing it from her friend's shoulders. She still felt an intense guilt for what had happened. If she'd done the right thing and dismissed Tina's request immediately, she and Joanne would never have been near the canal and this kind man wouldn't be dripping on the pavement like a drowned rat. "Once we're in the taxi it'll be warm and I'll get the driver to turn the heat up."

11

Broad Street was thronging with people arriving for the start of an evening out. Young women, in short skirts and midriff revealing tops, flicked long, straight hair from their faces. Groups of males laughed and talked too loudly – the alcohol they'd already had loosening their inhibitions. The wet group of three became the focus of attention for the passing revellers and Olivia placed herself protectively in front of Joanne. Taxis were unloading rather than picking up and it took only a few minutes for a black cab to respond to Olivia's arm signal and pull up alongside them. Olivia thanked the man with the dog again and pushed the jacket back at him. She then ushered Joanne into the car. The driver frowned when he saw the state of her. He looked like he was about to protest.

"She could sit on that newspaper," Olivia suggested quickly and pointed to a crumpled broadsheet on the front passenger seat. "I'll pay you for it. And could you turn the heat up, please?"

The driver muttered something about not needing the heat on in June but he flicked the switch anyway and passed the newspaper into the back of the taxi, Olivia arranged it on the seat and Joanne sat down. The car was soon too warm for comfort but Joanne didn't stop shaking. Her nose was running and her mouth was trembling. Olivia handed her a tissue.

"Fell in the canal, did she?" the driver talked into the rear view mirror. "That's what too much alcohol does for you. And it's early in the evening for being drunk. She's not going to be sick is she?"

"It was an accident and we're both sober." Olivia didn't give the driver any encouragement to make further conversation. She held Joanne's hand and wondered about her own fate. She felt like a tiny bug beneath Tina's thumb – with only the slightest effort Tina could effectively end her life. There had to be a way out, a way of making Tina think that Olivia had done as she was told. The evidence was there – there were now doubts in Joanne's mind about her relationship with Simon and Joanne had had a physical fright, even if it wasn't ultimately caused by Olivia. It all depended on Simon – if she could persuade him to reinstate Wayne then she would be off the hook.

The taxi pulled up outside Joanne's house. "What's the damage?" asked Olivia, pulling a couple of notes from her purse.

When they got to the front door, Joanne automatically felt for the strap of the bag on her shoulder and in that same moment they both realised the handbag containing her house keys was at the bottom of the canal.

"Shit!" Joanne started to cry, her nose ran again and she shivered and shook. It was imperative to get her inside and dried off as quickly as possible.

"You must keep a spare somewhere?"

Joanne shook her head.

"Not even with a neighbour?"

Still the negative response. Olivia muttered under her breath.

"Simon! I gave Simon a spare."

"Simon?"

Joanne was trying to mop her tears with the now sodden tissue Olivia had given her in the taxi. "He's coming round tonight and I thought I might be late because I was meeting you first. So I gave him a spare to let himself in. He should be here anytime now."

Both women looked hopefully towards the road and, as if on cue, a black Astra appeared, slowed down and stopped at the end of the drive in the place just vacated by the taxi. Simon slammed the door and the central locking clicked into place. He looked surprised when he saw the two women on the doorstep. Then his eyes rested on sodden Joanne.

"What's happened?"

"We need to get her inside and warmed up. Her keys are at the bottom of the canal."

"The canal!"

"Please, just open the door before she dies of pneumonia."

Inside Olivia instructed Simon to put the kettle on. She ushered Joanne upstairs and got her into a warm scented bath.

"As soon as I stop shaking and feeling wobbly, I'm going to ask him for my keys back and suggest we cool it for a bit." Joanne's voice sounded stronger as she began to relax and warm up.

"No, don't do that." Olivia turned round from her hunt in the airing cupboard for a bath towel. "Don't do that. I swear, I never saw him with anyone else. I made it up."

Joanne didn't seem to be listening. "I know you've got good judgement, Olivia. I trust you and you were married to him. I believe what you told me this evening and the last thing I need right now is a two-timing bastard."

Olivia was shocked at the venom her friend injected into the last few words. The seeds of doubt had been sown in her friend's head and it wasn't going to be easy to rip them back out. "But I just told you – I was making it up. Forget what I said. I did not see Simon with anyone else." Leaving her friend to soak in the hot water she went to brief Simon about the total cock up she'd made – and why. She wanted her friends to be happy again and maybe there was an outside chance she could also get Simon to reinstate Wayne. He didn't give her chance to speak.

"Tina's behind this, isn't she?" He was pacing the living room and spoke as soon as Olivia got to the bottom of the stairs. He didn't look at her. "She threatened something like this would happen if I sacked Wayne. But I never thought *you'd* do it. We couldn't live together as man and wife but I didn't think we were enemies. I thought we had an understanding. I thought we respected each other."

"Yes and no." Olivia grabbed Simon's arm to stop him marching backwards and forwards. "Tina wanted me to turn Joanne against you *and* give her a physical fright so you'd worry about her future safety and therefore do whatever Tina demanded, specifically reinstate Wayne in his job. I did the first and then came to my senses. I couldn't hurt her. An over-excited dog pushed her into the canal – not me. I swear I didn't do that."

"Turned her against me in what way?" Simon was holding Olivia by the shoulders now and looking directly at her. "What have you said to her? If you've destroyed us, I'll… I'll destroy you."

Olivia felt he would shake the words out of her if she didn't speak. She explained exactly what she'd said and what had happened and how she'd then tried to tell Joanne that the blonde woman had been a fabrication. "If Tina finds out that I didn't follow through, she may go to the police, the press or who knows where. I'll end up in prison."

Olivia could feel a lump building in her throat. Her chest felt tight and her eyes pricked. So far this evening she'd managed to stay in control but now she wanted to roll into a ball and sob. She closed her eyes and breathed deeply. Simon was still holding her by the shoulders. His grip was getting tighter. She opened her eyes and looked straight into his. He looked confused as well as angry.

"What do you mean – you'll end up in prison?"

Olivia realised far too late what she'd said and her brain wouldn't think quickly enough to retract the statement with a reasonable explanation. So she chose to ignore his words and cut to what was really important in order to get Tina off her back. "Will you take Wayne back on? If you don't, I think something really bad will happen."

"To Joanne?"

Olivia nodded, thinking as fast as she could. If Wayne got his job back then Tina would leave her alone. She could marry Mark and everyone would live happily ever after, including Wayne, who would be earning an honest living to support himself after Tina's death. Simon had to be made to reinstate him. "My clumsy actions tonight were only a warning. I'm guessing Tina might have connections with people who can do the job properly next time. She might know some proper criminals."

"I think we should just call the police and have Tina put away. We can't let this woman terrorise us."

"No! You can't do that." If Tina was dragged before the police, she would take Olivia with her.

"Olivia!" Joanne called from upstairs.

"I better make sure she's alright." The summons saved her from immediate further explanation and she scurried towards the stairs.

"Tell her that poisonous stuff you said about me wasn't true," Simon called after her. "Tell her I'm going to stay here, in her house until she believes me. I've never two-timed anyone in my life."

"OK, OK. You make some cocoa whilst I get her out of the bath and into some warm clothes."

Joanne had some colour back in her cheeks and she was lathering shampoo into her hair. "Tell me what's going on down there. I can hear raised voices but I can't make out what you're saying to each other."

"Just a minor disagreement," Olivia said, "I was going to stay the night but Simon insisted that it was his place to be with you and he's right. Like I said before, I lied earlier about seeing him with another woman. I didn't see him with anyone. He really loves you – and, believe me, I know when Simon is saying what he means."

There was a flash of hope in Joanne's eyes. "Should I let him stay?"

"Yes. I've done him, and you, an injustice this evening. Please don't let it cause any lasting damage between you. Simon will sleep on the settee. He understands you're shaken and he won't pounce on you in the night." Olivia wrapped her friend in a warm towel from the airing cupboard and left her to get dry.

"I'm phoning Mark now for a lift home," she said to Simon downstairs. "Any problems give me a call and I'll be straight back. I'm sure she'll be as right as rain in the morning."

"There's still something you're not telling me. What was that thing about prison?"

"That can wait. Joanne should be your priority now."

By the time Mark arrived Joanne was down in the kitchen, her hair wrapped in a towel and wearing a dressing gown. There was a mug of cocoa on the table in front of her. Joanne and Simon were eying each other warily, neither quite sure how to treat the other.

"What was all that about?" Mark asked Olivia as they drove away. "And why are the bottoms of your trousers wet?"

In her anxiety over Joanne, Olivia had forgotten her own legs were still damp from their brief dangle in the canal. "Don't ask. I was trying to get Joanne to think carefully before committing to Simon but I went too far with my warnings. She thought I was trying to warn her off completely. Then Joanne got knocked into the canal by an over-excited dog." She was surprised to find her voice was trembling. Any minute now she'd start sobbing. "But I want to forget all of that for now. How do you fancy a bottle of wine, a Chinese takeaway and an early night?"

Mark patted her heaving shoulders. "It must have been pretty bad to make you react in this way."

He was right. Now the immediate pressure was off Olivia was shaky and vulnerable. This evening had shown her the terrible depths to which she'd sink to protect her own back and she didn't like the person she'd turned into. It was like turning the clock back to when she was sixteen and had let someone else carry the can for her spur of the moment act of violence. She started to cry.

Olivia managed to squeeze her fiancé's hand before he needed it to change gear. Mark was a rock in her life and she couldn't bear to lose him. Whatever happened she somehow had to keep the truth about her past from him. He was much too nice to stay involved with a convicted murderer with a lifetime in prison in front of her.

***

Olivia's call came late when Tina was in the bath. She often had a bath before going to bed. Since she'd become ill the warm water helped her relax and sleep better.

Wayne called through the bathroom door. "Message from someone called Olivia. She says she's done what you wanted and the rest is up to Simon. Sis, is that Simon from the estate agents?"

"Yes, thanks." It was an effort to make her voice loud enough to be heard through the wooden door and the exertion set off a coughing fit. It was a couple of minutes before she could relax again.

She'd let Simon stew until tomorrow and then contact him about Wayne going back to work. It was a relief to know things were getting sorted. She'd been thinking again about the whole package for her brother's future. This job would help him massively financially but he also needed someone at home to look out for him. If his so-called mates got wind that he was earning a regular salary they wouldn't hesitate to take it off him in a card game each and every month. There had to be a way of getting him off this estate and away from all these bad influences. Sometimes she felt she was caring for an impressionable teenager rather than a fifty-year-old man. Her mother had been right when she'd asked Tina to find a nice girl for Wayne to marry. A woman was what he needed to give him stability. The difficulty was finding a woman who'd want Wayne. Having a job would make him a bit more eligible to the females on the estate but for the best chance of a good future he needed to be away from here. Even if a house move did temporarily upset his equilibrium

Wayne banged on the door. "Are you nearly finished in there, Sis? I need a pee."

Tina knew her brother's bladder was strong enough to last longer than the time she spent in the bath. It was his handwashing ritual that wasn't controllable and the kitchen sink wouldn't do if he was really anxious about something. His website mistake at the estate agents had upset him more than he'd admit and his anxiety was manifesting itself in a greater dependence on his rituals. "I'll be out in five minutes."

When she unlocked the bathroom door in her navy dressing gown with a towel wrapped round her hair, he was stood outside wringing his hands. He side-stepped past her and locked the door behind him. She heard the taps turn on immediately. When he came out he was much calmer and offered to make them both a cup of tea.

12

Simon failed to sleep on Joanne's settee. It was too short to allow him to lie down properly and he ended up with his knees uncomfortably bent up towards his stomach. His head rested on the arm and gave him an agonising crick in the neck. He considered creeping upstairs to Joanne's bedroom to check she was alright and then maybe quietly lying beside her in comfort for a bit. But that would be invading her territory, without her permission. By booking the redecorating she'd intimated she was almost ready for a closer relationship and he didn't want to jeopardise that future any further. So he remained on the settee and tried unsuccessfully to empty his mind of a plethora of confusing thoughts about Olivia's involvement in Tina's schemes. It didn't make sense, Olivia didn't owe anything to Tina – so why was she carrying out the woman's nasty schemes? It had been Simon's mother who had made the promise to Tina in prison, so it was he, if anyone, who owed the debt of gratitude, not Olivia. And why had she mentioned going to prison?

As a faint grey dawn began to filter through the gap between the curtains and the wall he decided he would phone in sick to the office. Joanne wasn't going to be in a fit state to go to work and she'd probably be grateful for the company, plus he wanted the chance to put things right between them. He wasn't sure exactly what Olivia had said to her to bring his faithfulness into question but there was going to be a lot of bridge-building to be done – and he wanted it complete as soon as possible.

Then he must have fallen asleep because he woke suddenly at the sound of footsteps in the house. He knew immediately where he was. Joanne must be up. The living room was now bathed in early morning sunshine. Olivia had provided him with two blankets before she left the previous evening. One of these was on the floor and the other had wound itself round his legs leaving his chest naked and chilly. Simon glanced at his watch, it was seven am. He pulled on the jeans and T-shirt which he'd abandoned on an armchair and ran a hand through his hair. He felt grubby and in need of a toothbrush and shower.

"What the…!" Joanne spun round from the kitchen sink and dropped the kettle on the draining board. "You made me jump!"

This morning she was wearing only flimsy cotton pyjamas which became almost transparent when the sun caught them. The thick, full-length dressing-gown of the previous evening was gone. Her hair was flattened on one side and there was a bit sticking up on the top. It reminded him of a teletubby's swirly aerial. His heart ached with love. He walked towards her, raised his arm and gently flattened down the wild hair. Joanne stood motionless and tense. Their relationship had gone back several steps and he was going to have to prove himself all over again.

"Sit down. Let me make you a cup of tea." He filled the abandoned kettle and placed it back on the base unit. He moved around the kitchen locating mugs, teapot, milk, sugar and teabags.

Joanne didn't move, her eyes flitting around the room after him. Simon stirred two teaspoons of sugar into her mug and tried to hand it to her. She refused it by keeping her hands by her sides. "Look me in the eye and promise that you've never been unfaithful to me."

Simon put the mug down and took her hands. He looked her in the eye. "I promise I've never been unfaithful to you."

Joanne nodded as though accepting what he said. He passed the mug to her and she took it. "I don't take sugar," she said.

"Yesterday was a shock. That's what the sugar is for. I've put some in mine too."

She held the mug in her right hand and then put her left on its smooth porcelain side, forming a circular hug around the cup. She had her wedding ring on. He'd never seen her wear it before. It attracted his attention like some protective talisman that announced 'I'm Not Available'.

"Are you after my money?" she asked curtly. "Roger had life insurance but it hasn't made me rich. You're barking up the wrong tree if you think you can live off me."

"Joanne, I am definitely not after your cash."

"There's no smoke without fire. Why did Olivia say those things about you being unfaithful and a gold digger? She changed her mind quickly but why say them in the first place if she didn't have suspicions about you? Or was she talking directly from the unpleasant experience of being married to you?"

"I was never unfaithful to her either. She had money when we divorced but I asked for none of it." Simon continued to look Joanne in the eye. These were statements of fact and she had to believe him. "Who knows why she acted like she did yesterday? She's hyper-protective of you because you're her best friend. She's got a lot on her plate with the wedding coming up. She's having all those weird nightmares and is exhausted half the time. Perhaps because our marriage didn't work she feels an odd responsibility for anyone else who gets involved with me. Maybe she wants you going into the relationship with your eyes open instead of sailing in blind like she and I did as youngsters."

Joanne sipped her tea, her eyes suspicious over the rim of the mug.

"Only the two of us can make our relationship work," Simon said. "Olivia may feel a responsibility but it's nothing to do with her. It's our joint responsibility to decide whether we will be good together. I think there's something special between us and I'd like to carry on trying. What about you?"

She hesitated. Simon braced himself for a putdown. Their hopes, fears and life experience hung heavy and silent between them.

It was a full minute before Joanne answered the question. "Yes, but slowly. More slowly than before. And right now I need some time on my own to assimilate what happened yesterday."

"Absolutely." He drained his mug and put it next to the sink. He was disappointed they weren't going to spend the day together but knew it wasn't wise to push his luck by attempting to persuade her.

Back at home he realised his mobile was still on the little coffee table next to the settee at Joanne's house. He called work from the landline and tried to sound sick rather than exhausted after an emotionally charged night. Immediately Rachel expressed concern about him. "You sound terrible, Simon. Your voice is all weak and shaky. Go back to bed. There's no way you should be in the office."

Simon was only too pleased to take her advice. He drank a mug of hot, sweet coffee and, when he felt calmer, he went to bed and slept until late afternoon. The phone woke him.

"Do you see now that I keep my promises and carry out my threats?"

Simon's brain was still half asleep and it was a couple of seconds before he registered the identity of the caller.

"What do you want?"

"I guess your cosy little love nest is rapidly disintegrating. Has she lost trust in you yet?"

Simon remained silent. He didn't want Tina to have the satisfaction of knowing that his relationship with Joanne had gone backwards.

"I arranged that little fright in the canal for your girlfriend."

"I know. Olivia told me." He didn't mention that Olivia had had second thoughts and it was actually a dog that knocked Joanne into the canal.

"Olivia also put doubts in Joanne's pretty little head about your suitability as a partner. And if Wayne isn't back working in your office tomorrow with a 5% pay rise under his belt, then next time Joanne won't just catch a chill and a chunk of fear. She'll be hurt much more badly. You don't think my brother's good enough for the important work in your establishment and I can't argue with that. But people with different strengths and weaknesses still need to be given a chance to earn their own living, even if it's only making tea and sharpening pencils – but on a living wage. Think on, or next time your girlfriend will be waking up inside the pearly gates."

"You're mad!" Simon's fists clenched. "I'm going to call the police and put an end to all this harassment. That letter from my mother doesn't give you permission to terrorise us."

"Calling the police is not a good idea." Tina's voice was icily calm. "I suggest you ask Olivia why the police should not be involved."

"Just tell me what's going on!"

But all he got in return was the ending of the call. He kicked his shoes across the hallway, banged his fist against the wall, threw his head back and cursed at the ceiling. Then he fetched the whisky bottle and slopped amber liquid into a tumbler. He emptied the glass with a couple of swallows and then coughed.

Tina was more ruthless than he'd imagined. Her botched attempt to extort money from them in the coffee shop had screamed, 'Amateur!' but now she'd upped her game to a scary level. She had some sort of hold over Olivia. A hold great enough to persuade Olivia to turn on her best friend and give Tina the leverage on Simon that she needed. How could his mother ever have befriended a monster like this? How could she have made a promise to this bitch and expected Simon and Olivia to keep it ad infinitum? If he let Wayne back into the office his own career reputation would be in shreds. Word had gone round all the local agencies about the mess up Wayne had made. Simon had taken a lot of teasing about it. If he allowed Wayne back he'd become a laughing stock but if he didn't, who knew what horrendous thing would happen? And it wasn't just him that bad things might happen to. More importantly he had to consider Joanne too.

He drank more whisky. Its fiery warmth stopped him shaking. He had a third large glass in the hope of reaching clarity of thought. He either took Wayne back or he called the police. The police were the obvious option but he remembered Olivia's distress last night. Maybe he should first give her the chance to explain Tina's hold over her and what she'd meant when she mentioned prison. But not now – he would give her the respect of talking to her sober.

***

Dean was waiting on the college wall as usual. Suzanne resisted the temptation to run the last few metres and fling her arms around him. With his mates hanging around, he wouldn't thank her for that. Dad had told her to un-ask the wedding invite but he didn't understand – she couldn't do that. She would look ridiculous – as if she was still a little girl without an independent life away from her parents. Plus Dean had asked her to go shopping with him to choose something to wear for the wedding. If she un-asked him she'd lose that whole afternoon of his company and the chance to put her influence on the stuff he bought.

"Hey!" Dean held up his hand. Suzanne did the same and they hit in a high-five. "How you doin'?"

"Good. Everything's good."

"What about the university thing? You knocked that on the head yet?"

"I'm… exploring other options."

"That's good. Shall we go to the park?" He took her hand.

This was good. Suggesting the park meant that Dean wanted to be on his own with her and he was always much nicer when he was away from his mates. It was as though a macho front dropped away from him and he became a real person.

"What did your parents say when you told them university wasn't happening?"

"It's not a definite decision yet." Suzanne chose her words carefully, anxious not to alienate him but also she didn't want to tell an outright lie. "Dad's not happy."

"Take no notice. You've got to live your life, not him."

Sometimes Dean said very profound things – she loved the way he could be surprising like that. Most people didn't get to see that side of him. If Dad could see it, he'd probably like him.

"I think Olivia would be OK about it, as long as I have an alternative plan. Mum was distracted when I told her. She's got a lot on at work and she wasn't really listening to me."

"It must be tough having, like, three parents to please. You've just got to show them you're grown up now and don't need them poking their noses in all the time."

Dean was right. With this university thing Dad was trying to live her life for her. She had to show him she had a mind of her own and she could do that by letting Dean come to the evening do without permission. Once he was there Dad wouldn't dare to cause a scene and it would show him that she could run her own life.

"You still OK for shopping tomorrow?" she asked him.

"Yeah, me nan's given me some money. She said to get

102

something that could be for job interviews as well as a wedding. I'm gonna need to find a placement soon."

Suzanne squeezed his hand and felt proud. Dean wasn't the loser some people, like her dad, might imagine.

13

Simon could hear the sleep in Olivia's voice when he called her the next morning. "It's Saturday..." she started to protest.

He didn't bother with apologies or small talk. "How did she make you do it?" Anxiety gave his voice an unintentional sharp edge. He was in a hurry to get the Tina business over and done with, the longer he delayed reporting the woman to the police, the bigger the chance that something else would happen to Joanne. "What did you mean when you talked about going to prison?"

"It was nothing. I was upset about Joanne. I exaggerated things and must have given you the wrong impression."

He suddenly felt lighter – there was no reason not to get the law involved. "I'm going to call the police now. Tina has to be stopped from hurting us further. I guess they'll want to talk to you about the canal but neither I nor Joanne will put any blame on you. We'll tell them the truth – that is, you couldn't go through with it." Simon had thought about it and this was being fair to everyone.

For a few seconds there was no response from Olivia. It sounded as though she was moving around. Simon heard a door close. When she did speak there was a slight echo to her voice as though she was in the bathroom.

"No! Don't call the police. Please, don't."

He didn't understand the panic in her voice. "I have to. Wayne is not having his job back and I'm not risking Joanne getting hurt again."

"If you tell the police, she'll…" Olivia's voice tapered out.

"What is this hold she has over you?"

"I can't…" The rest of her words were lost in sobbing.

This was ridiculous. He had to know what was going on. He had to talk to Olivia face to face. "I'll come over after work and you can tell me. Or better, tell me now."

"No, you can't come here. Mark doesn't know. And I can't tell you on the phone. It's too… personal. You'll be angry, upset, lots of things – I can't guess how you're going to react. Please can we just leave it for now? No police? Let me get the wedding out of the way before opening this can of worms."

"I can't wait that long. I don't want Wayne back in the office. I want the police involved. You *have* to meet me today." His voice reflected Olivia's hysteria. He tried to tone it down and put his point of view calmly. "I thought we each knew everything there was to know about the other. We went through so much together and we've managed to stay friends. Please don't shut me out now. Something is terribly wrong. Let me help you."

Olivia gave a resigned sigh. "OK, but please don't go to the police before we've spoken. I'll be at your house at 5pm – you shut early on a Saturday, don't you? It's my hen night so I can't stop long. And after you've heard what I've got to say, you'll probably call the police anyway."

Throughout the day Olivia's words bounced round Simon's head. He couldn't keep his mind on the pieces of paper that came over his desk. He forgot to return calls to clients and forced himself into a long walk at lunchtime in an attempt to gather his thoughts. What terrible thing was Olivia was going to tell him? What could she possibly have done to give a petty criminal like

Tina a hold over her? Were they both part of a drugs cartel or an organisation receiving stolen goods? Why else would Olivia think that he would call the police?

She was punctual but not her usual self. There were shadows under her eyes and she appeared tense and on edge. The constant nightmares must be taking their toll.

"Tea? Coffee?" he asked.

"I'd love a whisky but I'm driving."

Simon raised an eyebrow. Olivia liked a glass of wine but he'd rarely known her want spirits and never so early in the evening.

"Dutch courage," she answered his unspoken question.

"It must be bad. So, tell me then."

"Sit down. You're going to be shocked."

Simon took the brown leather armchair next to Olivia's. His shoulders wouldn't relax and there was a growing ball of apprehension in his stomach. Olivia moved her lips and looked like she was about to speak but no words came out. Her hands were clasped tightly in her lap.

She took a deep breath and frowned. "There's no easy way to say this so I'm just going to blurt it out, OK?"

Simon nodded bracing himself for a bullet.

"It was me that stabbed your father. Your mother was innocent."

Children shouted in the street. The letterbox banged and a boy with a fistful of leaflets passed the lounge window on his way to the next house. Somewhere, far away, a car alarm emitted a constant, faint wail. The door of a white van opened across the street and thumping, heavy bass music escaped. The hands on the clock were motionless.

"Say something!" demanded Olivia.

Nothing in the lounge had changed. Everything in its place and a place for everything. Except in his brain. His internal memory spool was unwinding rapidly, like a broken cassette tape.

"Well?" she asked again.

"I don't… I can't…" His personal history had turned upside down. His mother was *not* a murderer. Instead, the woman in front of him, the mother of his child, had killed his father. She had killed the man who, despite his vicious faults, would have been the grandfather of their child. And she had let an innocent woman take the blame.

"Rant and rave! Tell me what a scumbag I am. I let your mother rot in jail. You can't call me any worse names than what I've already called myself over the years."

"How could it happen? When I came down the stairs Mum was kneeling over my father. Her hands were on the knife." Simon spoke slowly with his eyes shut, trying to remember the detail. He'd pushed the memory away so often it was difficult now to see the sequence of events. Difficult to sort the real from the imagined. "I think you were in the corner. You looked terrified. I thought you were scared because of what my mum had done."

"I was terrified. I'd just murdered a man! Your mum took control of the situation and made the evidence look like she'd done it."

"Why did Mum take the blame?"

"She thought she'd get off more lightly because she was a battered wife. When she was on remand she wrote me a letter telling me to keep quiet and that she'd be out soon. She told me to look after you. So I kept quiet. But of course they gave her a much longer sentence than expected and the appeal wasn't successful. By then it was too late to tell the truth. Then I married you, which is what she wanted – at least she had the satisfaction of knowing that."

Simon needed a drink. Badly. But he couldn't get out of the chair. It was as though a trap door had opened in his head and his mind was plunging through a bottomless void. Everything was out of his control. He was dropping past the multi-coloured events of his past – but now they were all lies. "Did you marry me to make up for the guilt of getting my mum locked up? I thought you loved me."

To Simon, the pause before Olivia answered his question was far too long. It told him he'd said 'I do' to a woman who didn't love him.

"To be honest I don't know exactly why I married you," she said at last. "A big part of it was doing something exciting in Las Vegas. And I liked you. I've always liked you but also, I've always felt that I owe you something."

Simon became aware his nails were digging into the upholstery of the chair. Olivia's last sentence was hurting him far more than the revelation that she was a murderer. He'd been under the illusion that their marriage had been happy until David died. Admittedly, the baby had turned their lives upside down. The two short months of his life had been stressful and without sleep. They'd argued a lot but weren't things tough for all new parents? Simon was sure they'd have pulled through as a family unit if David had lived. He'd always thought it was only David's death that had driven them apart. Now Olivia was intimating that she'd only married him out of duty and that fact tore into his heart in the same way the knife had entered his father's chest.

A car went by outside. Someone shouted a greeting to a neighbour across the street. For most people life was going on as normal. For a few, life would never be normal again.

"Were you absolutely certain it was the right thing, when we got married?" Olivia asked. "Had you thought it through?"

"Of course I had. I wouldn't propose to a woman unless I loved her enough to want to spend the rest of my life with her."

"But we didn't exactly plan the wedding, did we? We were in Las Vegas and there were the wedding chapels. It was a spur of the moment thing. And my mum and dad had only been dead a few months. My emotions were up and down like a yo-yo."

Her parents' car accident had come only a week after the

engagement. The police had turned up on the doorstep as Simon was dropping Olivia off after a night-out. A drunk driver had ploughed into her dad's car. He'd been killed instantly and her mother had died a few days later without regaining consciousness. That was why they hadn't gone ahead with planning for a big church wedding. There didn't seem any point – they were both only children and the only surviving parent, Simon's mother, was in prison. "We were already engaged before your parents died. I thought that being engaged meant people loved each other enough to get married."

"For most of my life I've been worried about you finding out the truth about that night." She was changing tack. His emotions raced to catch up. "I've tried to imagine how you might react and this isn't how I thought it would be."

"What?"

"I thought you'd go ballistic over the fact that I murdered your father and then let your mother take the blame. Instead you're re-hashing our failed marriage. The fact that I caused the death of both your parents doesn't seem to come into it."

"To be honest I don't know what I'm talking about or what I think." Simon closed his eyes and ran a hand through his hair. "And how does all this tie in with Tina and her threats?"

"She knows what I did. Apparently your mum wrote it down as part of a creative writing exercise and it fell into Tina's hands along with that letter she showed us. If I don't do what Tina says she'll take that piece of paper to the police. She's got nothing on you so she's using me as a lever to get you to re-employ Wayne, however useless he is, so that he has a steady income when she's dead. That's what I meant about me ending up in prison." Her voice shook on the last sentence and she looked close to tears.

"Go to your hen night." He couldn't cope if she broke down. There was too much to assimilate. And there was a decision to be made. "I need to be alone… to think."

"My future is in your hands." Her words were a shrunken whisper. "What will you do?"

"Go away, Olivia! I don't know what I'm going to do."

"Don't shout at me." Her voice was desperate and her face pleading. "Please, at least consider taking Wayne back. Please don't go to the police."

"Go away!" He couldn't stop the sharp loudness of his voice.

Olivia scuttled out of the house. A few seconds later he heard a car engine jump into life. He listened to it grow quieter and then fade completely. The children were still playing and somewhere a dog barked. A lingering smell of perfume was the only sign that Olivia had been in the house.

His ex-wife had just admitted to him that she killed his father and let his mother rot in prison for the crime. She had asked him not to go to the police. Instead she wanted him to carry out the wishes of the woman blackmailing her and give an imbecile a job in his office. His ex-wife had also told him that she married him out of duty not love.

The obvious action was to go directly to the police, clear his mother's name and put an end to all the nonsense that had been going on. It would pave the way for a happy future for him and Joanne. Olivia's past was her problem.

Simon poured himself a large whisky and downed it in one. It sent a warming sensation down his throat and through his body. He refilled the glass and took another large gulp. His mobile was on the table in front of him. He could make the call now and draw a line under things. He picked up the phone and swiped the screen with his forefinger. Olivia had seemed so happy when they got married. She'd been skittish with excitement. There'd definitely been no sense of duty in the air. They'd both been overwhelmed with joy when the pregnancy was confirmed and the day they'd brought David home from hospital she'd never stopped smiling. He was convinced she must have loved him even if, with the distance of time, she couldn't remember it herself.

Simon tapped on the image of a phone handset. A number pad appeared and waited for him to give the digits.

The letter Tina had produced from his mother had upset him. It was typical of his mum to think of helping others no matter what her own hardships. His conscience pricked. Anything he did now was too late to help either of his parents but if Olivia went to prison, his mother's suffering would have been in vain. He believed Olivia's account that his mother had told her to keep quiet but it didn't make what she'd done right.

The screen in his hand had gone black. Simon put the phone down. Then he picked it up and swiped through to a picture of Joanne. His heart constricted at the thought of more bad things happening to her. One chance, he would give Olivia and Tina one chance to sort out whatever was going on between them. After that, for the sake of Joanne, he was out.

14

"Where've you been?" Mark called from the kitchen when Olivia walked in the front door. "I thought you'd be primping and preening before your hen night."

Olivia was still feeling shaky from her encounter with Simon but she couldn't let it show. "Got held up and I'm off to do that very thing now," she shouted from the hallway with false brightness in her voice and then went straight upstairs without facing her fiancé.

In the bathroom she stripped off, stood under a very hot shower and squeezed her most expensive shower gel liberally. The trauma of that conversation with Simon had to be expunged. She needed to become the excited bride-to-be enjoying a last fling with her girlfriends. But the anxiety was like a stubborn stain and it wouldn't wash away. After fifteen minutes it was still there in the pit of her stomach like a coiled snake ready to rise up and bite. Now there were two other people alive, plus her, who knew the truth. That meant two people who might report what she'd done: a big chance that she would end up behind bars before her wedding day. And only two weeks to go until she walked down the aisle.

The hen night was being held early because a few of the girls couldn't make the following weekend and after that it was too near the big day to risk late nights and hangovers – Olivia was of an age where her face needed time to recover from a heavy night. She dressed hurriedly, glancing at her watch. Mark had nipped out to collect Suzanne from her mum's – as a bridesmaid she was to be allowed to come to the earlier part of the evening, with Mark collecting her at 11pm.

"When you pick her up, don't come inside the restaurant," Olivia had warned him. "It'll be bad luck if you do. The husband-to-be isn't allowed at the hen night."

Olivia did her makeup and, with bright lipstick in place, experimented with a few smiles, pouts and grins. The bottom half of her face looked happy but her eyes were still anxious, like a sad clown. Maybe the first couple of glasses of wine would do the trick and allow her to forget the tightrope she was now walking between freedom and incarceration. She had hoped Simon would understand and empathise with the danger Tina posed to Olivia and offer Wayne his job back. Given the way Simon had screamed at her to leave, that wasn't going to happen. All she could do was wait to see which of them went to the police first, Tina or Simon.

The front door banged.

"Are you ready?" called Suzanne. "The taxi's just arrived."

"Two minutes!" Olivia put a comb through her hair, added more lipstick and then gave the mirror her best fake smile.

She'd booked a side room in the Italian restaurant and the others were already there when Suzanne and Olivia arrived. There were silver helium balloons bobbing on the table between the menus and wine glasses, the smells of several female perfumes mingled into one pleasant scent and there was much chattering and laughing with absolutely no volume control. The restaurant called it a side room but it was more of a giant alcove with the missing wall open to the main bar and eating area but it did contain some of the noise and disturbance from exuberant parties like their own.

"Here she comes – the blushing bride!" someone yelled.

There were squeals of delight and Joanne appeared with a pink sparkly sash, which she carefully lowered over Olivia's head and arranged diagonally from shoulder to waist. 'THE HEN' it proclaimed in bold silver lettering.

Olivia went tense and tried to read her best friend's facial expression. It was the first time they'd met since the canal incident forty-eight hours previously. She hadn't known whether Joanne would turn up tonight or not. She still didn't know if she would be missing a bridesmaid on her big day. Olivia had called several times but her friend had never picked up and Olivia had left grovelling messages begging forgiveness.

"Thank you for coming," Olivia whispered. "I don't deserve it."

"No, you don't." There was a harshness to Joanne's voice that Olivia hadn't heard before. "But if I hadn't turned up there'd have been questions and I'm not good at lying or feigning illness. And I don't want the whole world to know what poison you said to me about Simon, least of all, Suzanne, who'd already made me promise to sit next to her."

"Thank you, thank you. You're the best."

"Don't grovel. Smile and pretend everything's OK."

"Will you still be my bridesmaid?" Olivia took a breath and stared over Joanne's shoulder, bracing herself for a negative response.

Joanne fiddled with the sash, needlessly rearranging it on Olivia's shoulder and hip. She didn't lift her head to meet Olivia's eyes. "As I said, I don't want people to know how badly you treated me. Simon intimated there was some complicated reason behind it all but to me, the lies you told about Simon were unforgivable. There was some redemption in the fact that you were prepared to come into the canal and save me. So I'll still be your bridesmaid but I doubt I can ever be your best friend again."

That last phrase hurt but where there was communication

there was hope. That hope would be smashed when the truth came out and the police arrived, but for now it was enough. Olivia wanted to hug her friend with gratitude but feared such a gesture of affection wouldn't be well received at the moment. Instead she gave Joanne's upper arm a squeeze. "Thanks."

Joanne gave a tight smile and moved away to where Suzanne was waving from the other side of the room.

"Prosecco, madam?" A waiter in a white shirt and black trousers and smelling faintly of garlic was at her shoulder with a round tray of filled champagne flutes.

Olivia was confused. "I didn't order this."

"The lady just leaving now." The waiter spoke in stilted English and inclined his head towards the door of the restaurant. "She pay."

Olivia looked in the direction he indicated. A woman in a mustard suit opened the restaurant door and glanced back at the alcove before stepping out into the street. Unwillingly Olivia caught her eye and Tina gave her a grin and thumbs up sign before disappearing.

"Did she say why?" A cold finger of fear was wrapping itself around Olivia's heart.

"She say: one good turn deserves another. I not understand. But it was a nice thing, no?"

Automatic politeness made Olivia agree with the waiter but her mind was trying to decipher Tina's message. She didn't want the woman's wine, the fizz contaminated her party with evil. But refusing it would seem churlish and demand explanation. Olivia hoped Simon had acted quickly and agreed to take Wayne back and this was Tina's way of saying thank you to Olivia. Fingers crossed.

They sat down at the long table laid out with a starched white cloth, baskets of bread rolls and square butter pats in golden wrappers. Beneath the balloons, silver and pink sprinkles created a sparkly trail down the centre of the table. Olivia drained her glass of Prosecco and somebody poured her some more. She began to feel jolly. As the alcoholic bubbles burst, the cares of the last few days rose from her shoulders and drifted away, like the helium balloon down the end of the table which had come adrift from its moorings.

Catherine from the office ordered two more bottles of bubbly. "My treat," she said, "for the best boss I've ever had."

The kind words made Olivia blush with pleasure as she accepted the first glass from the new bottle. Then she glanced down the table, remembering Mark's request to make sure Suzanne didn't overdo the alcohol. His daughter wasn't yet seventeen and he didn't want her getting a taste for it. Olivia had agreed to be responsible but secretly she thought he was being over protective. In a little over a year Suzanne would be away at university and it was better she had some experience of the effects of alcohol now, before she was enticed into the excesses of the student union. That was if she went to university – Olivia had been surprised at the teenager's sudden wish to 'explore other options'. She wondered if the boy Suzanne had mentioned inviting to the wedding was involved in this about face. She must find time to talk to her about it when her brain could accommodate problems other than her own. Suzanne was sitting next to Joanne, who was topping up the girl's champagne flute with orange juice. Seeing she was in safe hands, Olivia relaxed and decided she was going to enjoy this evening.

Menus were passed around but everyone was too busy talking and laughing to wade through the list of pastas, pizzas and salads. Three times the waiter came over hopefully with his pad and pencil and three times he was sent away because they hadn't yet decided. He was beginning to frown and look at his watch. Olivia dug her glasses from her bag and tried to concentrate on what she wanted to eat but the wine and giddy company was making her mind wander. Looking around it seemed that no one wanted the hassle of making a decision either.

"Please could you bring us a selection of starters?" Joanne had taken charge. "Then six different pizzas, three pasta dishes and two large side salads."

The waiter was nodding gratefully and scribbling with his pencil. Olivia gave Joanne a smile of gratitude. Her ex-best friend looked away.

They'd reached the coffee stage and were arguing over the last foil-wrapped chocolate mints when Olivia spotted the blue uniforms. Two policemen were talking to the man behind the bar. At first, in her slightly drunk state, Olivia thought they'd come for a takeaway to eat in their patrol car. Then the hairs on the back of her neck rose and anxiety uncoiled with alacrity in her stomach. The barman had pointed them in the direction of their side room and the two men were walking over with obvious purpose.

The smaller of the two men removed his helmet and bent to speak to Catherine who was sitting nearest the bar area. His voice carried. "I'm looking for Olivia Field. Is she part of your group?"

Catherine giggled. "Police! I didn't know you were invited to the party. She's our hen. She's over there, in the pink sash. You're not going to arrest her, are you?"

An expectant hush had fallen over the group and the last sentence carried like a tannoy announcement. Everyone was looking at the blue uniforms. A car horn sounded outside. Olivia felt as though she was watching a slow motion film. She saw Joanne nudge Suzanne and point out of the window.

"Let me stay just ten more minutes. Dad won't mind waiting." Suzanne's voice floated down the table.

Olivia was aware of the police hovering at her shoulder. Her heart thumped and she felt the beginnings of damp under her arms. Had Simon contacted the authorities? She didn't want either Suzanne or Mark to witness her arrest.

"I think you should go now, Suzanne." Joanne's voice was

firm. "If your dad comes inside for you and sees Olivia, it will be a million years bad luck. He's fifteen minutes late anyway, you should have been gone already."

"But he'll see her when she gets home later."

"That's different. You must go outside before he comes in."

Thank goodness, once again, for Joanne. You could tell she'd already been through the teenaged daughter thing twice with her own. The police were whispering between themselves but Olivia knew their eyes were on her. From the corner of her eye she could see the silver glint of handcuffs hanging from the waist of the taller policeman. There was a baton too. Please let them wait until Suzanne was clear of the premises. Please. This was a moment she'd feared all her adult life and finally it was here. They were going to take her away. She would spend the rest of her life locked up.

Something snapped in her head. She couldn't sit back and let this happen. Too much was at stake. She stood up. "I'll come with you, Suzanne. It's been a long day, I'm tired and…"

There was an almost imperceptible nod from Joanne to the smaller policeman, the one that seemed to be taking the lead. He stepped forward.

Traitor! It was Joanne who had called the police. This was the real reason her so-called friend had turned up tonight. She wanted to witness the arrest that she'd instigated. Joanne had wanted to stage manage tonight and have Olivia arrested in the most humiliating way possible.

"Please sit down again, madam. I can't allow you to leave." There was a heavy hand on her shoulder forcing her back down onto her chair.

Glancing sideways Olivia could see the waiter make a gesture of incomprehension at the barman who also shrugged. Probably no one had been arrested on these premises before. Now Joanne was almost pushing Suzanne out of the door. There was the noise of a car engine starting up. The policeman had a hand on each of her shoulders. Joanne walked back over to their alcove and gave that nod again. The officer moved his hands, one gripped the bare flesh at the top of Olivia's arm and he pulled her upright. They were standing close and she could smell the spice of his aftershave. She could see the beginnings of stubble on his chin. His breath smelt of toothpaste.

Her stomach was churning. She was desperate for the loo but didn't dare say anything. There was silence around the table. Everyone must be able to hear her heart banging against her ribs. The policeman brought out the handcuffs. Olivia began to tremble. Any minute now he'd caution her about remaining silent or the possibility that her words could be used against her in evidence. She would say nothing until she had a lawyer present. Her stomach was churning with the large meal she'd just eaten and the alcohol she'd drunk. She tried to focus on avoiding further humiliation by not throwing up. The officer snapped one half of the handcuffs around her right wrist. She gasped. He fastened the other half onto the left wrist of the taller policeman. Olivia's knees buckled. It felt as though the blood was plummeting from her head to her feet. She saw her friends around the table through a purple mist and it was impossible to focus. There was a sharp, painful tug on her wrist with the handcuff as she went down.

15

"Olivia! Olivia!" Someone was repeatedly slapping her face.

She opened her eyes. A folded jacket was pushed beneath her head.

"It was just a faint." Catherine's face was looming over her. "She's OK. No need to call the ambulance."

"Thank God. I would never have forgiven myself." Joanne's voice sounded distant.

Someone helped her to sit up and she was aware of Joanne walking away. The waiter handed her a glass of water. She took a gulp and then the memory hit her like a bullet. Her hand shook too much to hold the glass steady and water slopped into her lap. The police! She looked at her wrist, the handcuffs were gone.

"The police?" she asked.

Catherine gave her an odd smile. "At the bar. I was as surprised as you. Joanne had to explain. The others knew already."

Renewed humiliation crept over Olivia. So much for Joanne not wanting the others to know how badly Olivia had treated her. She looked over to the bar where the officers were talking to Joanne. The taller one was rubbing his wrist as though he was in pain. The handcuffs, when she hit the deck, must have been a dead weight dragging his arm down to the floor. She fingered the red mark around her own right wrist. Joanne handed something to the shorter man. It was too small and distant for Olivia to see what it was. Possibly the proof that Tina had talked about? That piece of writing Audrey did in prison?

"I'm really sorry. I didn't anticipate she'd react like that." Joanne's voice became audible as she looked towards the alcove. "But you're not out of pocket."

Then, from her seated position on the floor, Olivia watched her friend's strappy sandals walk alongside the men's heavy, dark shoes to the door. "She's usually up for a laugh. But I'll be sure to show her your website so she knows what we all missed tonight. Believe you me – the rest of us are really disappointed."

"Maybe we'll get chance to reveal all another time?" The policeman had a flirtatious voice.

Joanne laughed. Olivia frowned. Events had moved beyond her comprehension. The police seemed to be trying their luck with her friend and there'd been no arrest.

Catherine helped her from the floor onto a chair. "We're all devastated, Olivia. Underneath those uniforms lurked two of the best male bodies ever known to womankind. The others trawled hundreds of websites to find them. Then you go and faint and we don't get to see even a tiny morsel of male flesh!"

Olivia tried to understand. "I… who…"

"They were male strippers." Joanne placed another glass of water on the table next to her and handed her a napkin. "Dry yourself off with this. We paid an arm and a leg for a bit of titillation from the hunkiest men in the Midlands. Then you keeled over and we had to send them away – with our money but not one photo on our phones for Facebook."

Olivia was drowning in a wave of relief. "Thank goodness. I thought…" She couldn't stop the tears pouring down her cheeks. She put her arms on the table and rested her head, trying to hide her emotion.

"What did you think?" Joanne sat down on the next but one chair, leaving an empty seat between them.

"Nothing… it was nothing." Olivia blew her nose and tried to shake herself back into party mode. "Shall we order more wine?" She looked round for her friends but there were only the three of them left.

"It sort of killed the atmosphere when you keeled over. Didn't seem right everyone hanging around after that."

"And I'll be off now." Catherine pulled on her jacket. "See you at work, Olivia. And glad you're feeling better."

Despite her protestations that she felt fine, Joanne insisted on accompanying Olivia home in a taxi. "It's what the others would expect a best friend to do. I'm doing it for the façade."

It was their second taxi journey in three days but this time Joanne was in charge of directing the driver. Then she turned to Olivia. "Why did you react so badly to the police uniforms? You were as right as rain until then."

"I just felt weird – too much stress in the lead up to the wedding?" Olivia tried to keep her voice light. "Combined with too much alcohol?"

"It wasn't anything connected to the other night was it? When you decided it was time that Simon and I went our separate ways."

"That wasn't what I said and I took it all back anyway."

"The seeds of doubt were sown."

"No, it was nothing to do with that." Olivia glanced across the car seat and saw the doubt in her friend's eyes.

"I don't believe you, Olivia."

***

Tina woke up feeling better than she had in a long time. Physically there was no doubt that she was going downhill fast but this morning her mood was buoyant. Simon had called the previous evening and said he'd give Wayne another go at the estate agency. It was a shame he hadn't been gracious in defeat but he had given Tina the triumph of victory.

"OK, send him back to the office," he'd said in a weary voice. "I'll find something menial that even he'll be capable of."

"I knew you'd see sense in the end. Frightened of your nice girlfriend getting hurt again?"

"Something like that." Then Simon had ended the call.

Feeling magnanimous in her victory she'd treated Olivia to fizzy wine for her hen night. She wanted to spook the younger woman and let her know that Tina wasn't going to quietly disappear. She was going to keep Olivia on her toes and possibly use her services again. The alcohol had a cost a lump of her remaining shoplifting stash but the feeling of power had been worth it.

Slowly she levered herself out of bed and pulled her towelling dressing gown on, tying the fabric belt in a rough knot. It was the first dressing gown she'd owned. On her initial admission to hospital it became obvious that she needed something to cover her pyjamas and her modesty. Wayne had been despatched to get something suitable and had come back with this navy blue affair that was a size too big and getting more and more spacious as Tina lost weight.

She put the kettle on and made toast. It was serendipitous that as her physical strength deteriorated she'd found another, much stronger, power. The power to manipulate people. Tina smiled at her reflection in the kitchen window. This new power made her feel good. She felt confident for the first time in her life. Influencing the actions of others was giving her a high – a feeling much better than alcohol, cigarettes or the little bit of dabbling in drugs she'd done when she was younger. She was a puppet master, pulling the strings of Olivia and Simon. This must be how politicians felt when they swayed millions of people to vote one way or the other. Now she understood some of the truth behind that phrase, 'power corrupts': Tina's success so far at controlling Olivia and Simon had sparked another idea, an idea that would absolutely guarantee Wayne's future when she was gone. She rubbed her hands together in pleasure. When your days were numbered, life happened in a brighter technicolour and a shorter timespan, the brain sharpened, confidence grew and, above all, immediate actions counted – there wasn't time to sit back and contemplate the rights and wrongs of a particular path. But preparation was still important. Olivia wouldn't be happy with Tina's new idea. She would fight against it. But that written proof of Olivia's guilt meant there'd be very little wriggle room for her. Her compliance would be almost guaranteed.

Tina had left Audrey's papers on her bedside cabinet so they wouldn't go walk about in one of Wayne's clean sweeps around the lounge. She'd noticed they were still there a couple of days ago when her neighbour had brought round a pile of old magazines for her.

"Something to flick through when you're not feeling too good," the woman from across the landing had said. "Keep them for when you've had a bad day at the hospital."

Tina had put the pile down by her bed, on top of Audrey's letter and the account of the murder.

Now she went to re-read that account. She liked holding the paper in her hand and skimming over the words. It had the power of a loaded gun. But the bedside table wasn't how she remembered. The pile of magazines had shrunk to only one and there was only bare wood beneath that magazine. No letters or papers. She flicked through its pages urging the single sheet of paper to fall out. She held it by its spine and shook. Nothing. Perhaps the sheets of paper were already somewhere down on the floor. It was an effort to get herself down to carpet level and peer under the cabinet and under the bed. Her joints creaked and complained. In his new role as master cleaner, Wayne hadn't even left a stray dust ball in the under-bed gloom, let alone a sheet of paper. She opened the cabinet cupboard door. Perhaps he'd shoved them in there. She found nothing but her medications.

Her brother must have moved the papers. Please don't let him have destroyed them. She took deep breaths and tried to calm herself. Audrey's written account of the murder was Tina's power. Without that piece of paper she was nothing.

"Wayne!" she shrieked.

There was a thump and a bang from behind the plasterboard wall of the adjacent bedroom. Seconds later he appeared in the doorway. His remaining, thinning hair was tousled with sleep. His bare chest sported a thin vertical line of hair between his man boobs. His stomach hung jelly-like over the top of striped pyjama bottoms.

"What's matter, Sis? Are you ill?" The concern etched on his face was deep and genuine. "Why are you on the floor? Did you fall?"

He took hold of her arm to help her up from the kneeling position but she shook him free.

"There was an important piece of paper 'ere." She banged the cabinet with her fist. "And now it's gone."

"I… tidied up yesterday. I know you said not to move your stuff but I… I thought it would make up for me getting the sack. But I don't remember no paper."

"So where did you put the stuff from here?"

"It was just magazines and I… I don't remember… they might have gone down the rubbish chute. I looked at the dates on the magazines so I didn't chuck the newest. It was wrong to use the chute, I know, they should've gone in the paper recycling box – but I couldn't be bothered." Wayne looked ashamed.

"I don't care about recycling. I need that piece of paper!" Tina's heart was thumping and she had to concentrate on her breathing. She couldn't shout because her lungs had to suck in the air they needed. "Without that paper I have no power to make Simon keep you in a job. Without that paper I can't put my second plan into action."

"I'm sorry." He sounded like the small boy from years ago, pleading for forgiveness from their mum when he broke a china rose that had been a present from their grandmother.

"OK." She sighed. What was done, was done. There was nothing to be gained by labouring the point. "You can help me up now."

Wayne took her arm and her knees creaked again as her legs unbent from the kneeling position. As soon as she was safely sitting on the bed, Wayne fled for the bathroom. She heard the door lock and the taps turn on and off several times. Tina didn't count but she was sure it was more than usual – she'd obviously upset him.

Tina spent the rest of the morning drinking tea made by a repentant Wayne and doodling on a piece of paper. By lunchtime she'd decided it was worth giving her second plan a try, even without her best weapon. She would pretend the paper still existed. The prize would far outweigh a dogsbody job in an estate agents and there was no risk. Olivia would never go to the police because she had far more at stake than Tina. Thus far Olivia hadn't asked to see the written proof left behind by Audrey. If she did, Tina could pretend it was hidden away in some bank vault. If Olivia decided not to play ball, Tina could still go to the police and tell them what she knew – she might not be believed but it would at least arouse suspicion and hang a question mark over Olivia's character.

She watched *Pointless* on early evening TV with Wayne and cheered her brother's general knowledge as he shouted at the TV, comparing himself favourably to the contestants.

When it had finished she muted the volume of the *News at Six*. "I've got you a date for tonight, Wayne."

"What?"

"I know a lady who's looking for a serious relationship, probably marriage."

"With me?"

Tina nodded and watched Wayne's expression change from shock to a broad grin. "Have a shower and smarten yourself up. Then I'll explain more."

When she could hear the electric shower raining into the bath she called Olivia.

"That was excellent work you did manipulating Joanne and Simon for our own gain. I hope you enjoyed the bubbles I provided for your hen night? They were just a token of my thanks."

There was a grunt in response.

"It was nothing, really, no need to thank me," Tina said sarcastically and smiled with satisfaction. She'd only spoken a few words and already she had the upper hand in this conversation. She didn't need a piece of paper to give her power. "Now I have an extra special treat for you. It's a treat that will last a lifetime."

Olivia grunted again.

"You're a woman of few words today, Olivia. But no matter, I just wanted to let you know that Wayne will pick you up from your house in exactly sixty minutes. He'll be in a black cab. You're going on a date."

"What?"

Tina smiled at the hysteria in Olivia's voice. "Don't worry, love, he brushes up very well. He's in the shower now and I'm pressing a shirt for him. He won't show you up."

"Go to hell! I wouldn't be seen dead with your moron brother."

"That's a bit harsh, Olivia. You hardly know him."

"I won't be going out with Wayne!"

"I'll ignore that comment. Are you going to tell your fiancé that you're seeing another man just before the wedding? Or shall I?"

There wasn't even a grunt this time, just silence.

"Wayne has a heart of gold. He has some annoying habits too – but which of us don't? Anyway, he'll make a loyal and loving husband. You're in the market for a husband and he's in the market for a wife, a match made in heaven I'd say. And you've already had a hen night so you're well on the way."

The line went dead. Tina smiled – Olivia wasn't going to get off the hook by simply ending the call. If Wayne married Olivia, Tina could die happy. Wayne would be secure for the rest of his life and Tina could meet her mum in the next life knowing that she'd kept her promise. There was the small problem of Olivia's current fiancé but that wasn't insurmountable.

16

Olivia's mouth was dry and her heart raced. Surely Tina and Wayne didn't expect her to go along with this ludicrous plan? Mark was in the next room expecting her to spend the evening with him. Tonight they were going through the Venice guidebook and picking out the sights they'd like to see on their honeymoon.

She took a couple of deep breaths and tried to compose a 'normal' facial expression. Tina's telephone call was a stupid, idle threat, made purely to spook her. Wayne wasn't about to turn up on the doorstep. She poured two glasses of red wine and went into the lounge. Mark had a tourist map spread on the coffee table, a paperback book open in front of him and he was tapping at a brightly coloured site on his iPad. Everything was normal.

"I think we should book a guided city walk for day one," he said without looking up. "That'll help us get our bearings before we try exploring on our own. I'm just booking it now. But we also need a rough itinerary for each day so we don't waste time."

Mark always liked to be in control and have a plan. Sometimes he needed reining in to avoid a holiday becoming too regimented. Olivia wanted some chill-out time too, for simply enjoying the company of her new husband.

"How about some time on the beach?" she pointed to Lido di Jesolo on the map. "It'll be hot enough for swimming and sunbathing."

"OK, I'll timetable that in along with the Guggenheim and Doge's Palace."

Olivia sat next to him on the settee and put her head on his shoulder. Sometimes he irritated her with his lists and plans but he kept her on the straight and narrow. It was rare for something to go wrong if Mark was involved. He always had a backup plan, which was why he was so successful in his career as a project manager. Compared with the prospect of Wayne, Mark seemed very precious indeed. She put both arms around him.

"Hey! What's brought on all this affection?"

"No reason, other than I love you and I can't wait for us to be married." She felt a sudden desperate longing to become his wife as soon as possible – once that ring was on her finger it would be harder for Tina to plot and plan.

"Me too." Mark kissed her head. "Now on this map—"

Olivia's phone trilled. She glanced at the display: Tina. "Sorry I've got to take this." She rushed into the hall, closing the lounge door behind her. She spoke in an angry hiss. "I refuse to go out with Wayne. I played along with you by putting the frighteners on Joanne and lost my best friend. I refuse to lose my fiancé as well. Are you trying to snatch my whole life?"

"An eye for an eye – you snatched the life of one person and left the other to rot in jail. Your penance is devoting your remaining days to my brother. Anyway, in a few seconds you'll hear Mark's phone ring. That will be me. I'm looking forward to telling him where his fiancée is going tonight and who with."

Olivia's brain whirled. "How did you get his number?"

"Some work receptionists are more helpful than others. Speak later."

A minute later she heard Mark's phone through the lounge door. She rushed in. "Don't answer it!"

He ignored her and swiped his finger across the screen. "Mark Nugent speaking."

Olivia grabbed the phone from him. "You've made your point. I'll be ready."

"I knew you'd come round to my way of thinking."

Olivia ended the call and pushed the phone back at Mark, her brain galloping to find an excuse. "I have to go out. That was an ex-colleague who has a 'thing' about me. We went out a couple of times a while back. I finished it but he's never accepted it." She was gabbling. It was impossible to control her words. "He heard on the grapevine that I was getting married and has been calling me. I've stopped taking his calls so now he's taking a different tack. He got your number through your work."

Mark looked shocked and confused. "That's stalking. We should get the police involved."

"No need." She took a breath and looked at Mark's face. It was obvious from his expression that he believed her ex-colleague story. "I'll meet him in person tonight and put him straight."

"But this is harassment. Stalkers turn into murderers. Let me come with you – that way he'll really get the message that it's time to back off."

"No. I'm not a child. I'll deal with it myself." Wayne would go ballistic if she turned up with her fiancé. "I'll make sure he gets the message that I'm not available."

"Wear something frumpy and don't bother with makeup."

Olivia looked at her watch. "There's not enough time to tart myself up even if I wanted to. He'll be here in a few minutes."

"He knows where you live!"

"It's pretty common knowledge at work. I've been here for fifteen years and have had the odd party or two."

Mark stood up and gently took hold of her shoulders. His

eyes were full of concern and looking into them made Olivia want to pour out the whole story. She didn't want to keep secrets from her future husband but Mark would never marry someone who had stabbed a man. If she told him, she would lose him forever. Olivia didn't know if she could cope with Wayne tonight or put a stop to what he wanted from her but she had no choice but to try. The thought of him touching her, as if they were on a proper date, made her feel sick.

"Be careful, Olivia. If you are at all scared, give me a call. You are going to a public place, aren't you? Is your phone fully charged?"

Olivia nodded. She had no idea where they were going but the fear in her throat made speaking impossible without the sobbing starting too.

A car horn sounded outside and they both jumped. "I better go."

Mark followed her to the front door. As she got into the taxi next to Wayne, Olivia pasted on a bright smile, turned and gave her fiancé a wave. She kept the artificial grin until the house was out of sight.

***

Wayne was disappointed. Olivia had made no effort to dress up for their date. Her hair was sticking out at one side, her makeup was tired and her clothes looked crumpled from being worn all day at work. Tina had convinced him that Olivia was keen to spend the evening with him but she wasn't giving that impression now. She sat as far away from him as possible and stared out of the window. She hadn't even acknowledged him when she got into the car.

"We're going to The Black Sheep," he said, trying to get her interest. "It's a pub in the country with a beer garden and they do food. It'll be lovely on a warm night like tonight."

Olivia didn't turn round. She seemed to find the passing shops and businesses more interesting than him.

"Have you been there before?" Wayne had done the rituals seven times before he'd left the house. He had transferred his mother's photograph into the pocket of his best trousers. Tina had impressed upon him that this date must be a success and so he was leaving nothing to chance. Now the important thing was to keep the conversation going.

"No."

He needed a new subject to talk about, something that women were interested in.

"Are you going somewhere nice on holiday?" The woman who cut his hair each month was always asking this question. It got the female customers talking about the sun tops and strappy dresses they'd bought from Primark for their fortnight in Spain.

Olivia turned from the window and stared at him. Now he'd got her attention he smiled. Maybe she was as nervous as him and had been looking for a conversation opener too. She was gripping her handbag tightly and looked a bit twitchy.

"I'm going to Venice on my honeymoon in a fortnight." She looked at him accusingly, as though this was something he should know.

Wayne opened his mouth but no words came out. He shut it again. Tina had told him Olivia's relationship was on the rocks. Tina was rarely wrong. Olivia must be having second thoughts about the wedding otherwise she wouldn't be here with him tonight. He had to ignore the remark about the honeymoon and plough on.

"That's nice," he managed.

Olivia returned to looking out of the window. The taxi pulled up in the pub car park. Wayne paid the driver and got out. Olivia didn't move. Wayne suddenly realised what she was waiting for, dashed round to the other side of the taxi and opened the door. She didn't thank him but that was probably her nerves again.

"Shall we sit outside?"

She shrugged. He took that as a 'yes' and they walked around the outside of the building to the grassy area at the back. He put his hand in the small of her back, like he'd seen men with beautiful women do on TV. She sidestepped away from his touch and he was disappointed. There was a children's playground with a few youngsters climbing, swinging and spinning. Beyond that was a nice view over open fields. Wayne thought it was romantic.

"You choose the table," he said.

Without looking around, she sat down at the nearest one. He noticed sadly that she put her handbag on the bench next to her so he would have to sit opposite rather than close to her. Maybe she was shy of new men. Hoping she might mellow after a glass of wine, he went to get the drinks. The food menu was chalked on a board behind the bar. Wayne was shocked when he saw the prices. The money in his wallet would only stretch to two helpings of Shepherd's Pie and not even that if they had another round of drinks. He didn't know if Olivia was expecting to eat. Tina hadn't said or given him any extra cash. He could manage on a pack of crisps until he got home but he couldn't let Olivia go hungry.

"Do you want anything to eat?" Some of the wine slopped over his wrist as he put her glass down heavily on the wooden slatted table.

She shook her head. He felt relieved and tore open the pack of salt and vinegar crisps and placed it between their glasses.

"Help yourself. Or I can get another flavour if you want?"

She shook her head. He put a handful of crisps in his mouth and licked his fingers. A shower of crumbs drifted down and sat on his dark trousers. Had she noticed the mess he'd made? He didn't brush the bits away for fear of drawing attention to what he'd done. Was there a posh way to eat crisps? They sat in silence. People at the other tables were talking to each other and laughing. One couple were even kissing. He glanced at Olivia. It was obvious from the set of her face that it was much too soon for kissing.

She looked miserable. He felt sorry for her and her unhappiness with her fiancé. But why didn't she just break off the engagement?

A dog came over and he held out a couple of crisps on his hand. Dogs weren't allowed in the flats otherwise Wayne would have had one. The animal snuffled greedily and then put his head in Wayne's lap, trying to vacuum up the crumbs. Wayne tried to stand up to push the dog away from him but the table and bench trapped his thighs. His legs jolted the wooden structure. Olivia's reactions were quick and she saved both glasses before they lost more than a few slops.

"Thanks," he said. "Tina's always telling me I'm clumsy and she's right."

They sat in silence again. He could think of nothing to say.

"This is never going to work, Wayne." Her fingers were drumming on the table and she took a large drink of wine.

"What?"

"Me and you, together. I'm very happy with my fiancé. I don't want anyone else."

A cold disappointment squeezed him from within. He'd known it was too good to be true when Tina had told him about the date. Nobody ever wanted Wayne for the long term. The rituals put them off. But Olivia didn't even know about the handwashing and the photograph. She just didn't like him, full stop. Maybe he wasn't likeable. The screaming and laughter from the children's playground drew his attention. He wished he was still a child, life was so simple back then. He didn't used to get anxious when he was a kid and he still had his mum to look after him.

"I have to go to… to the gents.'" He gripped the table and extracted his legs from their trap. The toilets were empty and he managed to wash his hands seven times with no one else seeing. As he walked back through the pub he fingered the photograph in his pocket. If he stopped to do the photograph ritual properly Olivia might disappear and it would be like waking up to real life after a nice dream.

"Let's call it a day and go home." Olivia was picking up her bag and getting ready to go when he got back to their table. "I'll call a taxi."

This was his fault. Tina always said he should try harder. In her eyes he never did anything right. He'd tried so hard with the cleaning but had thrown away the important piece of paper. He'd tried so hard at the estate agents but had got the price wrong. Wayne really wanted to do this right and make Olivia love him. She was pretty even when, like tonight, she'd made no effort to dress up. Her face looked soft and he wanted to stroke it. She hadn't drawn the thick black lines around her eyes that lots of the women on the estate did. Olivia looked more like a princess than a woman from the estate.

"No! We can't go home." His voice came out too loud and Olivia looked scared. She sat down again, putting her bag on the table. Wayne was worried that he'd upset her. Without thinking, he leaned across the table and put his hand on her bare arm. She pulled it away.

"Looks like you two lovebirds are getting on great." Tina appeared from nowhere with a full pint glass. She took the seat next to Olivia. "I won't stay long. First dates can be awkward and I wanted to make sure you were giving it a fair chance and not scarpering off home early."

Neither Olivia nor Wayne spoke. It was one of the rare times that Wayne wanted to send his sister packing. Her turning up on their date like this would make Wayne look an even worse proposition than he already was in Olivia's eyes.

"Good job I came, I can help the conversation along. I've got a friend who had an arranged marriage," Tina said. "She's from India. She hated the bloke at first sight. And I can confirm he's not got any better looking with age. He reminds me of a toad – short and fat with bulging eyes. But he's a caring husband and she's happy. He's always earned a good wage, been generous with his money and helped with the kids. She's never had to work. Instead she's been a housewife and looked after both sets of parents. It's been a win-win situation and it goes to show that first impressions can be wrong. The most unlikely pair can make a great team when they pool everything."

"That's a sweet tale," said Olivia, "but I'm sure Wayne doesn't want to be stuck with me for the rest of his life. I'm not the home-making kind and I've already got a fiancé."

"Marriage to you is absolutely the best thing for Wayne. You can give him the financial and emotional security that he's never had – the security that I won't be able to give him for much longer."

"But why would Olivia want me?" Wayne spoke to the table. He didn't like all this talk going on as if he wasn't there.

"Olivia has a big dark secret. If it's leaked she'll be locked away for a very long time. But if the two of you get married the proof will never get to the police. Again it's a win-win situation for both of you. Enjoy the rest of your evening, lovebirds. I'll book you a table to go out for a meal tomorrow night." Tina finished her pint and strolled out of the beer garden.

"Another drink?" Wayne pointed at their empty glasses.

"Gin, please." Olivia's voice was a whisper. "Make it a double. Here's the money." She pushed a ten pound note across the table.

Wayne hesitated. He didn't want to appear as if he only wanted her money. Whatever Tina had said, he wanted to marry for love. But he was low on cash…

"You might as well take it. There's no point you losing too much on the evening."

He pocketed the note and headed to the bar, wondering if she'd expect the change. When he came back he put the coins on the table in front of her, being careful not to drop them through the slats. Jeremy Kyle said honesty in a relationship was good. Olivia didn't pick the money up and they didn't speak. She was staring into the distance and Wayne didn't know what to say. She drank half the gin in one big gulp.

"Will Tina carry out her threat?" Her right hand still gripped the glass.

Wayne nodded. You always knew where you were with Tina. She did everything she said. Olivia finished the rest of the gin quickly, coughed and blew her nose. Wayne was scared she might cry. He touched her arm again, this time she didn't pull away.

"Do you want to go home?" He'd hardly touched his second pint but it was worth the sacrifice if he could make Olivia feel better.

She nodded, picked up her handbag and manoeuvred herself out from the bench. She appeared to have forgotten about the money on the table. He picked up the pound coins and put them in his pocket.

In the return taxi the gap between them was smaller. Wayne felt she wasn't as angry at him as she had been at the start of the date. Tomorrow at the restaurant he'd try even harder. Tomorrow he wouldn't allow himself to fail. When they pulled up at Olivia's house he wondered whether to leap out and open her door. But she was out of the car before he had time to react. She didn't look back as she went up the garden path. For a wild and heady moment Wayne wondered what it would be like to live in that big smart house with her. Maybe he'd be able to have a dog of his own. Then a curtain twitched and a man peered into the growing darkness through a downstairs window. It must be the wicked fiancé. Wayne looked away quickly.

17

"How do you think it went last night?" Tina watched her brother use the glass measuring jug to pour exactly the right amount of milk onto his cornflakes. He shovelled a spoonful into his mouth and then spoke, exposing the half-chewed contents.

"She didn't want to be there." Wayne wiped his hand across his mouth to catch the escaping milk.

"Did you want her to be there? Do you like her?"

"Yes! She's the classiest bird I've ever known."

"So don't let her escape tonight. You haven't got time for a long courtship. Tonight you have to persuade her to leave that poncy fiancé."

Wayne didn't know how to do that. He had nothing to offer but himself, which wasn't much. Tina had talked about Olivia having a dark secret but he didn't want a woman to marry him because his sister had blackmailed her into it.

***

Olivia hadn't told Mark she was going out again. They were both shattered. The nightmares had stalked her continuously the previous night and after the third one she'd cried in Mark's arms for a full five minutes without being able to tell him why. She'd prayed the promised second date with Wayne wouldn't become a reality but Tina had phoned twice in the last hour. When Olivia ignored both calls, the woman had texted a threat to ring Mark again. Olivia had no choice but to reply immediately with a message of acquiescence. A minute later her fiancé arrived home from work.

"Mark! I'm sorry. I was going to call you but work's been manic. I forgot to say I'm going out tonight." She watched the frown travel from a deep crease in his forehead down the rest of his tired face. "Can you get yourself something out of the freezer to eat? I'll be back as soon as I can."

He removed his shoes and placed them together on the mat inside the front door. He hung his jacket on the end of the bannister. His silence and the set of his shoulders told her he was angry. Finally, he spoke. "Can't this socialising wait until after the wedding? My sister's waiting for a verdict on which towels you want as a present. The hotel was on the phone earlier about the finger buffet menu for the evening disco, which we still haven't finalised. We didn't finish the Venice stuff and the photographer wants a list of what group photos we'd like. A mere man like me can't make these decisions alone." The last sentence was meant to be funny but there was no humour in his voice.

"No, it can't wait." Was her voice too tetchy? "A couple of the girls from work want to take me out for a pre-wedding celebration. They couldn't make the hen night." It was incredible how the more you did it, the easier lying became.

"What if your stalker man's waiting somewhere? You'll be vulnerable if you're drunk and out with a couple of air-headed blondes."

Olivia didn't rise to the implied criticism of her work colleagues. "I told you – I got the message across to him last night and he won't be bothering me again."

"Getting rid of him didn't get rid of the nightmares, did it?"

Olivia ignored the barbed comment and Mark made several harrumphing noises. Then he went to root in the freezer for something to eat. The bad atmosphere didn't augur well for a couple with their wedding less than a fortnight away. Olivia silently promised to make it up to him as soon as the business with Tina and Wayne was finished. And it would be finished soon. It had to be.

Olivia's hands shook as she buttoned up her blouse and struggled with the catch on a brightly coloured necklace. Mark thought she was going out with friends so she had to dress up. Unfortunately Wayne would think she'd made the effort for him. She started her makeup. The skin beneath her eyes was getting darker each day. Before the nightmares took hold the previous night she'd lain awake trying to formulate a plan to foil Tina and Wayne. In each of her invented scenarios she stood up to the pair and refused any further contact with either of them. Each scenario ended with Tina going to the police and Olivia being sent down for murder or, in her rosier visions, for perverting the course of justice. There was no way out of this situation. She put gloss on top of her palest lip colour and used a squirt of spray to keep her hair in place.

When she went downstairs the kitchen door was half-closed and the microwave was whirring.

"See you!" Olivia called as brightly as she could. "I won't be too late."

She slipped on her shoes and was opening the front door when Mark rushed into the hall.

"I'm sorry," he said. "I shouldn't have moaned about you going out. Have a lovely time and there'll be another day to catch up on all the wedding stuff."

"No problem."

He moved closer, as if to kiss her. Olivia stepped back from him. He gave her an odd look but she couldn't cope with the close contact of her fiancé right now. His affection would release her tears and, more frighteningly, the story of her predicament. Her dark secrets would trash their relationship.

The restaurant Tina had booked was on the south side of the city. Olivia was glad – it reduced the risk of being seen by anyone she knew. Tina had insisted Olivia pick Wayne up on the way. She parked the car at the foot of a grey, concrete high rise block and texted to announce her arrival. Hooded youths eyed her car suspiciously. The girls that walked past wore skirts that were too short and heels that made them totter uncomfortably. The outer page of the free *Metro* newspaper was blowing along the path. Graffiti adorned the lower parts of the concrete walls. A row of empty beer cans was lined up beneath a wooden bench. This was all the culture Wayne had ever known. She and he were as different as chalk and cheese. Even if Mark didn't exist, it would be impossible for them to build a working relationship. She was sorry about Tina's illness but that was no reason for Olivia to sacrifice the rest of her life for Wayne.

***

Suzanne recognised the red Mini immediately. It had driven past them slowly, as if the driver wasn't sure of the route. The multi-coloured screen of a satnav was clearly visible on the dashboard. She and Dean had been sitting on his garden wall facing the road. When the number plate came into focus, Suzanne had ducked her head behind Dean's shoulders. Why was Olivia here on the estate? Had she found out about Dean and come looking for her? This was only the second time he'd invited her back to his house and Suzanne hadn't explicitly mentioned him to Dad, Mum or Olivia since the failed request for him to come to the wedding.

The first time Dean had brought her home had been after

their shopping trip on Saturday. She'd been really excited when he pulled her off the bus with him instead of letting her continue on home. He'd dropped her hand when they started seeing people he knew but she didn't mind. The very fact that she was on his home turf with him meant she was important in his life.

His mum had been watching TV.

"Mum, this is Suzanne, my girlfriend."

The words took her by surprise. Up to that point he'd done nothing to make her think their relationship was serious to him. That word 'girlfriend' made her grin from ear to ear and she felt warm inside. Despite the presence of his mother, she reached for his hand and he squeezed it in return. This made them officially a couple.

Dean's mum had turned the TV off. "I'm very pleased to meet you, Suzanne. Will you stay for tea?"

"Yes, please."

They'd had sausages, chips and beans followed by tinned fruit salad and ice cream. It was the sort of meal she never got at home. Then Dean's mum had to go out and they'd sat on the sofa, kissing, cuddling and watching TV until Suzanne knew she couldn't stay out any longer without causing trouble for herself back at home. Dean had walked her to the bus stop and kissed her goodbye in front of his mates. There'd been wolf whistles and grubby remarks. That had made her feel cheap but Dean had seemed to enjoy it and let his hands wander a bit further over her bottom than usual. He was showing off to them at her expense and she didn't like it. On the bus home she had clung to the fact that he'd called her his girlfriend.

Today, her second visit, Dean's mum hadn't gone out after tea so she and Dean had come outside. He'd said his mates would be along soon. The lads came into sight just before Olivia's car drove past and Dean had shuffled nearer to Suzanne on the wall, kissed her and put his arm around her. Then she saw the red

Mini and tried to squeeze as much of herself as possible behind Dean. She was sure Olivia hadn't seen her.

"Let's go meet them." Dean gestured at his mates who were coming towards them from the other side of the Mini. He pulled Suzanne down from the wall.

"In a minute." She bent down and fiddled with the laces of her trainers, playing for time and keeping her face hidden.

"Come on!" His voice was getting impatient and he gave her crouched bottom a little kick.

The lads were level with the Mini now and a fat man, followed by two other podgy looking blokes, was approaching it as well.

"Ow!"

Ignoring her protests, Dean was pulling her upright.

***

There was a hard rap on the window. Olivia jumped and glanced sideways. Wayne was waving and grinning at her through the glass. A couple of Wayne clones stood behind him. Each had a beer belly, low-slung jeans and tattooed arms. One had a shaved head. Behind them was a gang of teenage lads pointing at her car. Olivia felt vulnerable. She lowered the window only a couple of inches.

"These are me mates, Keith and Mick. They wanted to meet you."

Olivia nodded and smiled a false greeting. "We better get going, Wayne. The restaurant might let our table go to someone else." There was little chance of that on a Monday night but Olivia wanted to escape these thugs.

Tina had chosen a newly-opened restaurant which Olivia had never been to before. The menu had a European flavour and the food was excellent. The décor was sleek and diners were given privacy by the provision of booths. Mark would like it here. But she could never bring him somewhere tainted by the memory of Wayne. The evening was less awkward than the previous night because the food gave them something to focus on. Olivia wanted to pick Wayne up on his table manners but thought better of it. She said nothing as he ignored his knife and used his fork like a spoon, with the tines horizontal, to shovel in mouthfuls of coq au vin. Drips of the red-brown gravy spotted the white cloth around the edge of his plate.

Between courses he made a laudable attempt at finding some common ground between them. "What do you do for a living?"

"I'm in IT."

"Computers aren't my strong point."

She nodded, remembering Simon's description of Wayne's cock-up at the estate agency. There seemed little point in helping him out by responding verbally. He might assume that she was enjoying herself. She would just answer direct questions.

"What's your favourite soap, Emmerdale or Coronation Street?" he asked.

"Neither."

The waiter cleared their plates and frowned at the stained cloth. His eyes passed over both of them and it was obvious he was trying to work out why such an odd couple were dining together. He brought the dessert menu. Olivia declined and ordered coffee. Wayne went for sticky toffee pudding with custard. Before it arrived he went to the bathroom for the third time. He was gone several minutes and returned smelling of perfumed soap.

"Are you OK?" If the frequent toilet visits meant Wayne wasn't well, Olivia would happily suggest cutting the evening short.

"I'm fine." He looked at his hands instead of her.

When the pudding came he seemed relieved to find that the custard came in a separate jug and he could pour on just the right amount himself. He held his spoon like a trowel and demolished the sponge quickly, rubbing his belly with satisfaction when he'd finished. There was a thin ring of yellow custard around the outside of his lips. It turned Olivia's stomach but she said nothing.

Ordering coffee had been a mistake – it came after the toffee pudding and prolonged the agony of the evening.

"Do you only get them if you have coffee?" Wayne was pointing hopefully at the foil-wrapped chocolate mint sitting in her saucer.

Olivia nodded and handed him the mint. Wayne ate it and screwed the wrapper into a tight ball.

"Shall we go now?" Olivia had drunk the coffee as fast as the hot liquid would allow.

Wayne looked disappointed but didn't argue and started to remove his jacket from the back of the chair.

"We need to pay first," she said quietly. "You need to ask the waiter for the bill."

"Oh!" Before she could stop him, he walked to the adjacent table where the waiter was spooning vegetables onto the plates of an elderly couple. He tapped the waiter on the shoulder. "The bill, please."

Olivia cringed and looked in the opposite direction. The waiter nodded and indicated with his head that Wayne should sit back down again. They sat in silence for a few minutes while the waiter finished serving and then took an inordinate amount of time fiddling with the till and his notebook. Eventually he walked over and placed a piece of paper in front of Wayne.

"The bill, sir." The waiter hovered.

Wayne held the paper at arm's length, squinted and looked shocked. Then he produced several twenty-pound notes. Olivia thanked the waiter and told him to keep the change. Wayne opened his mouth as though to protest but Olivia met his eye and he said nothing.

"That's what's expected," she said as they walked out into the street. "He gave good service and deserved a tip."

She relaxed on the drive back to the estate. All that remained was to drop Wayne at the flats and then go home to Mark. He'd be waiting up for her. She was glad he'd apologised before she left the house – there'd be no bad atmosphere to return to. Her chest swelled with a sudden rush of love for her fiancé. Very soon she'd be one of those 'smug marrieds' that Bridget Jones wrote about in her diaries and she couldn't wait! This nightmare with Tina and Wayne would be over.

She pulled up outside the flats but kept the engine running. Around the bottom of the tower block were several low-rise buildings: dank, grey concrete cubes that served as houses.

"Would you like to come in for a drink?" Wayne asked as she waited for him to get out of the car.

"No, thanks. I've got to be up early in the morning for work. You do too, don't you? Now you're back at the estate agency?" Olivia willed Wayne to hurry up and disappear. Why did he think she'd want to prolong this charade by going into his seedy, little flat?

"I suppose so." Still he sat in the passenger seat wringing his hands as though there was something he had to get off his chest.

"I need to go home now, Wayne. Mark will be wondering where I am."

"I... I think we could be good together. Opposites attract and all that."

Olivia cringed at his words and wished there was an ejector button linked to the seat next to her. "No, never. We cannot be good together. I only came tonight because of pressure from Tina. Now I'm tired and I want to go home."

Wayne reached into his jacket pocket and pulled out a small penknife. He held it pointing towards her.

18

"Oh!" Olivia leaned away from Wayne and the threatening piece of metal. She pushed her back against the driver's door and tried to make herself into as small a target as possible.

"Give me the car key." There was a slight tremor in his voice. He was nervous and nervous people could be unpredictable.

Olivia's heart ricocheted back and forth. She considered making a run for it but there was a thug with a defecating Alsatian only five yards from the car. Wayne's hand was shaking and the little self-assurance he had, had disappeared. He leaned towards her with the knife in his right hand. Olivia was already pressed hard against the door and there was nowhere further to go. The smell of chocolate mint still lingered on his breath. Without warning, he scratched the skin of her neck with the knife.

She gave a yelp, turned the engine off and handed him the car key.

"I'm getting out of the car. You get out as well. If you run we'll catch you. He's me mate." Wayne pointed at the dog walker.

Olivia hesitated. Wayne scraped her skin again with the blade. The sharp pain made her wince. She touched her neck and examined her finger. There was a drop of blood. She got out of the car slowly. In a second he was at her side, holding her hand and smiling as though they were a courting couple. The knife was hanging in his free hand, mostly covered by the too-long sleeve of his jacket. Wayne nodded at a group of teenagers drinking out of cans at the grey entrance to the block of flats. A girl was in their midst. She had the hood of her sweatshirt up and her face turned away. She looked as vulnerable as Olivia felt.

"Have a nice night. Both of you," called the male nearest to the girl, giving Wayne a leery wink and a thumbs up. "Be good!"

Olivia cringed. Having Wayne simply squeeze her hand like this made her skin crawl, the thought of him doing more turned her stomach. Inside the flats they had the lift to themselves. It smelt sour. She didn't want to breathe. She tried not to think what activities went on in this metal box on a regular basis. People who couldn't wait to relieve themselves in various ways. She moved her feet; the floor and now the soles of her shoes, were sticky. Wayne stood too close, he dropped her hand and put his arm around her waist. Olivia tensed, turned her head away and stared at the graffiti. Someone had tried to clean it off and it had been reduced to dark pink swirls.

"We won't do anything you don't want." Wayne was talking to the back of her head. "But Tina says I have to win you over tonight. To do that we need to spend time together. That's why we're having a drink now. I make very good tea."

"If I don't go home Mark will call the police."

"Does he know about me?"

Olivia shook her head and stared at the floor. Eventually someone might spot her car outside but by then it could be too late. When the lift door opened she didn't move. He scratched her neck again and propelled her on to the landing with a hand in the small of her back. Whilst he was fiddling with his key in the door of the flat she started to run for the stairs. Despite his bulk Wayne reacted like lightening and caught her sleeve, pulling her back. He held her wrist tightly with his left hand

and unlocked the door with his right. She tried to twist her limb out of his grip but his hold on her was too fierce and she only caused herself more pain. The knife had disappeared. He pulled her into a dark hallway and kicked the front door shut behind them. It was a warm evening and the flat felt stuffy and smelt of stale cooking. He took her through into the lounge. There was a grubby, blue leather three-piece suite and a low glass-topped coffee table. The curtains at the full-length windows were open and framed a vista of coloured lights towards the city centre.

"Tina promised she'd go out tonight, until late. Just in case we… got friendly. I'll put the kettle on."

The kitchen area was reached via an archway from the living room. There was no door and Wayne was at the sink with his back turned. There was the sound of thorough handwashing. She was out of his line of sight. Olivia pulled her mobile from her handbag but she wasn't quick enough to send a message; Wayne turned round.

"Sugar?"

"No." She held the phone behind her back but it was impossible to text or call.

She was surprised to see him spoon loose tea into a teapot. Through the whole pouring, stirring and straining process he kept turning to face her, as though he didn't quite trust her. Olivia was thinking more coherently now. Even if she was able to use her phone behind her back, she didn't want to alert Mark to the lie she'd told about going out with the girls tonight. It would open a Pandora's box of trouble just for the sake of another thirty minutes in Wayne's company – he might let her go when they'd had this drink. She'd keep the phone out of Wayne's sight but within reach, in case things got worse.

"Had to wait for it to brew." Wayne brought two mugs over and put them on the scratched glass of the coffee table. The cup nearest Olivia had a pink lipstick mark on the rim. They both saw it at the same time.

"Shit!" Wayne looked mortified. "That's Tina just after she's put her lippy on. It don't come off easy in the washing up. Not unless you notice it and give it a proper clean. I always make sure I get it clean but Tina washed up today while I got ready to come out with you. I'll make you a fresh one in a clean cup." Wayne picked the mug up and started back to the kitchen.

"No! Don't bother, it'll be fine." The sight of the pink grease mark turned Olivia's stomach but the rigmarole of brewing another pot of tea would delay her departure even further.

"Drinking out of a dirty mug isn't nice."

"Really, I don't mind. I'll give it a clean with this tissue."

Frowning he put the mug back on the table. Olivia produced a tissue from her bag, spat on it, rubbed the mark away and tried not show her distaste. "It'll be fine now, she hasn't got the plague."

A wave of sadness passed over Wayne's face. "She has got cancer though, but that's not catching, is it?" He took a gulp of brown liquid. "I want her to live to see our wedding, it would make her so happy. So we need to hurry up."

They sat in awkward silence for a minute until Wayne spoke again. "Is that your phone behind you? Put it on the table before you lose it down the cushion and drink yer tea."

With her eye on the knife on the table in front of Wayne, Olivia did as she was told. It was her safety net snatched away. She turned the mug around, choosing the part of the rim furthest from where the lipstick had been, before taking a tiny sip. Wayne put his drink down, wiped his mouth with the back of his hand and gave her a big smile.

"We can watch TV, if you like. *Big Brother*'s on now or we can watch a film?"

"I already said I can't stay long. I have to get up for work in the morning."

Wayne moved nearer to her on the settee until their legs touched. Olivia tried to move away but she was already right up against the upholstered arm. The blue leather was ingrained with brown marks. He grabbed the remote control and started flicking through channels, finishing on a group of people lounging around a modern, minimalist room. The monotone of a narrator was describing them doing nothing. Olivia felt the warmth of Wayne's hand on her knee. She realised he saw the tea drinking as a prelude to something more exciting and not the finale to their evening. She stared at her phone, willing someone to call so she could snatch it up and alert the outside world to her predicament. The screen remained blank and silent.

She stood up. He grabbed her hand and pulled her back down.

"Sorry," he said. "I'm not used to… women." Despite his middle-age, Wayne's expression was a mixture of naivety and hope. "I don't know the best way for us to make progress."

For a second Olivia felt sorry for him but he was holding her in this grubby little flat against her will and she did not want to be the woman who advanced his knowledge of the opposite sex. "Perhaps next time." She lied and flashed him what she hoped resembled a warm smile. "But really, I must be going. I'm hopeless with late nights."

"No!" He was clutching at her hand. "Tina and our mum won't rest in peace until they know I'm settled down with a nice girl. They… I would like that nice girl to be you."

Olivia turned her head from the naked emotion in his face.

"If I let you go now and you marry Mark everything will be… messier and more difficult. You must stay with me. I have to do this for Tina. She has to die knowing I'm cared for. I won't let you go! I want her to die happy."

Olivia pulled herself free and stood up again. Wayne raised his bulk next to her. A new determination had appeared in his eyes. He slapped her across the face, hard. She was momentarily stunned. Her cheek smarted.

"I'm sorry." His face was full of remorse. "I shouldn't have done that."

Before she could react Wayne pulled her into a close embrace and his lips sought out hers. She could feel their rubbery dampness on her forehead, her cheek and then her mouth. It was a futile struggle to push him away; he was much stronger than her. She could smell a stale combination of tea, beer and chocolate mint on his breath. His arms roved down her back. She lifted a foot and kicked him in the shins. He winced but didn't loosen his grip.

Her phone rang. For a second Wayne dropped his arms and turned towards the source of the noise. Olivia grabbed the phone. The number wasn't recognised but she accepted the call.

"This is an important message regarding your mis-sold payment protection insurance. We can help you—"

"Joanne! Call the police! I'm being held hostage by Wayne at—"

Wayne grabbed the phone from her and listened.

"All claims will be treated…" The continuing recorded voice was loud enough for Olivia to hear.

"I might not be as intelligent as you but don't treat me as if I'm an imbecile." Menace had crept into Wayne's eyes. The pathetic 'love me' expression had gone.

Olivia was no match physically for Wayne. Her options were limited. If she made a run for the front door, he'd be on her whilst she was trying to work the lock. If she screamed, he'd have his sweaty hand over her mouth in an instant. She'd have to outwit him.

"OK," she said. "I'll be honest. It's not you I'm fighting. I like you but I'm trying to stay faithful to my fiancé. He'd be devastated if he knew I'd been with another man."

"He'll know soon enough when you call the wedding off."

"But he deserves to be treated with respect. Do you want to

be with a woman who discards her men more easily than her handbags?"

Wayne frowned. "I don't want you to leave me for another man."

"Exactly and I'm not the sort of woman who cheats on her man. Let me go home and explain to Mark that I'm not ready for the commitment of marriage. I'll tell him me and him are finished. That way I'll be free to date you without the guilt of being unfaithful and we can enjoy our courtship. You just need to give me a few days to sort everything out."

"But Tina said—"

"Never mind about Tina." Olivia took both Wayne's hands in hers, ignoring the way his damp palms made her skin crawl. "This is our relationship to conduct in a way that makes us happy. I can't relax and enjoy being with you if I'm feeling guilty. And I don't want Tina organising where and when we see each other. If we're going to date each other properly *we* need to be in charge. We're both adults and capable of conducting our own love affair."

"We're going to have a love affair!" Wayne seized on the last words. He stroked her hair and cheek. "I'm sorry I hit you. I've made your cheek red. You're amazing. I don't want to lose you."

Olivia tried not to recoil from his touch. "You won't lose me if you let me go now. I'll let Mark down gently and then you and I can be together forever."

"Promise? Promise we'll have a love affair?"

"Promise."

"I'll walk you to the car."

Going down in the lift Olivia put up with him holding her hand, touching her face and kissing her hair. When they got to the car he gently held her shoulders.

"Please kiss me before you go."

She couldn't argue and stood stiffly whilst he kissed her. She couldn't respond.

"Didn't you like that?" He looked disappointed.

Olivia shook her head. "As much as I want to, I can't relax and enjoy you until I've got rid of the guilt of Mark. After that, our love affair can begin." His face lit up again when she said the last sentence. As she drove off she could see him waving in the rear view mirror. Olivia's heart rate didn't drop back to normal until she pulled onto the drive outside her own house.

Mark was already in bed and half asleep when she got in.

"I tried to wait up but you're later than I expected. Good night?" he mumbled.

"So, so. I'm going to have a shower."

She turned the temperature up and let the hotter than usual water cascade over her body, washing away the lecherous feel of Wayne's hands and lips, the grubbiness of his flat and the terror of the evening. Mark was snoring softly when she got into bed. She wanted to tell him about Wayne and Tina. She wanted her fiancé to help her fight this threat to their marriage but that was impossible. The only person she could talk to was Simon because he knew her secret. She hadn't dared contact him since revealing the truth about the night his father died. He'd been devastated when she couldn't swear that she'd married him for love. Funny how lying to Wayne came easily but she hadn't been able to untruthfully soften the blow for Simon. Despite the hurt she'd inflicted, Simon had done as she asked and given Wayne his job back. She couldn't expect more help from him but if she didn't talk to someone soon she'd burst.

***

Suzanne had caught the last bus home from the estate. She'd arrived just as her mum was about to phone the friend Suzanne had used as an alibi for her illicit visit to Dean's. There'd been a lecture about staying out late on a school night but Suzanne had countered it by explaining they'd spent the evening doing homework together. Her mum had seemed satisfied-ish.

Now anxiety and indecision were keeping Suzanne awake. The anxiety was about Olivia. Why had she picked up the fat man from the estate and then, later, come back and gone into the flats with him? The Mini had still been parked outside when Suzanne left to catch the bus. She couldn't ask Olivia or her dad without giving away the fact that she'd been on the estate and her dad, especially, would go ballistic if he knew she was seeing someone from the council estate.

The indecision was about Dean. On his own he was great. He made her feel special and loved. And that tingly feeling when he'd described her as his girlfriend had been second to none. When they were on their own together she would give up everything to marry him and have his children.

With his college mates he was OK. They were used to her turning up after college now and she liked their banter. Dean wasn't lovey-dovey or proprietorial with her then, it was like she was a good friend. But he did hold her hand, which she liked.

On the estate he changed into a different person. He went out of his way to make sure the lads saw her and he made it obvious that she was his woman. She felt like a shiny trophy being held up for admiration. He touched and kissed her all the time. Sometimes in a way that was inappropriate for a public place. It was like he only wanted her there so he could show her off and improve his standing in the gang. When he was like this she wanted to run a mile, finish their relationship, go to university and make sure her life and that of her children was far better than that of the estate's inhabitants, who had no greater ambition than to get off with a good-looking bird or macho male.

Should she stick with Dean, because next year, when they both had jobs, they could rent a nice flat far away from the horrible estate influences? Or should she pack him in and go to university – and risk never finding anyone else to love her with her cushion tummy?

19

Simon stared at Olivia across the coffee shop table. Her makeup was heavier than usual but dark circles were still visible beneath her eyes. She gripped her tall latte glass with two hands as though trying to squeeze some comfort from it. Her early morning phone call a few days before had wrenched him from sleep. She'd whispered incoherently about Wayne and Tina and then ended the call abruptly, as though she'd been interrupted. Later she'd texted but still he didn't understand what was going on. He hadn't returned the call or the text. Perhaps he didn't want to understand. Perhaps he didn't even care about her anymore. Olivia wasn't the person he'd once thought she was. In the space of a few minutes she'd sullied the history of their marriage and destroyed her own good character. But still he felt a loyalty to this woman who'd once been his wife, this woman who'd shared the worst night of his life, this woman who'd given birth to his only child and shared the tragedy that followed. He remembered how Olivia's face had contorted with pain every time she'd pushed to bring David into the world. She'd taken huge lungfuls of gas and air and then pushed again, emitting a deep guttural groan as her muscles strove to bring their baby into the world. Each push had looked like it was a last supreme effort but each time she'd found the energy to push again. Then, in a second Olivia had gone from a wild woman convulsed in agony to a serene Madonna cradling her baby. Admittedly, she had been a mess, her face was red and sweaty, her hair was everywhere and the baggy T-shirt she was wearing resembled a smelly sack but beauty radiated from her. It had been the most wonderful scene Simon had ever witnessed. Cautiously he'd bent over and kissed his son's forehead and then his wife's lips. She'd rewarded him with a joyful smile. That moment, when the future had been unknown, had been perfect. It was because of that moment and what she'd gone through to give life to their son, that he couldn't desert his ex-wife in her hour of need.

"She's blackmailing me again." Olivia raised her head from the pale brown liquid and looked him in the eye. "Tina wants me to call off the wedding and marry Wayne instead."

"What? That's insane!"

"She is insane and I'm really scared. She's forced me on two 'dates' with Wayne already." Her fingers put the inverted commas around the word 'dates'. "He tried to hold me hostage in his grimy flat on the last one. He had a knife and look." Olivia pulled back the high collar of her blouse and Simon saw thin red lines, obviously the result of cuts made with a blade.

"Oh my God!" Simon shook his head disbelievingly. "I never thought she'd go that far."

Olivia let her collar fall back into place. "I've talked myself into a few days' respite from their attentions. But if I refuse to marry Wayne, Tina will go to the police about what I did to your father." She looked down for a few seconds. Then she raised her head and continued. "I would lose everything. Whatever I do I can't win." Her voice was brittle and words caught in her throat, as though she was about to cry. "Whatever I do, I'll lose Mark. He won't want me if I'm convicted and jailed. I can't talk to anyone but you. I don't deserve anything after what I did to your family but you have to help me. Please."

159

Simon had never seen her looking this desperate.

"How?" He touched her arm. "I've already done what you asked and reinstated Wayne at the agency. He's a liability, the worst member of staff I've ever had. The rest of the team are on the brink of rebellion but I know I can't sack him."

Olivia removed one hand from her latte glass and reached for his hand. "I appreciate what you've done, Simon. I've no right to ask for more – thanks for listening today. Just having someone to talk to helps."

For a minute or two they sat in silence holding hands across the table. He squeezed her hand, hoping to transmit some comfort.

"But what shall I do?" Her eyes were shining with tears. "I don't know what to do."

He felt he had to offer some sort of plan, no matter how flimsy and he said the only thing he could think of. "Make yourself uncontactable until after the wedding and don't be alone – ever. Only answer calls from numbers you know. Get Mark to take you to work and collect you – think of some excuse to persuade him. Don't go out by yourself or stay at home alone. And put some sugar in that coffee, that's guaranteed to make you feel better immediately."

Obediently, Olivia tore open a brown paper packet, poured the brown granules into her drink and stirred. She drank a third of the liquid and then dabbed her mouth with a serviette. "That plan might stop them kidnapping or contacting me but it won't stop them going to the police or telling Mark everything." There was still a shake in Olivia's voice and she glanced from side to side, as if afraid she might be being watched.

"It's all we can do for now." He took her hand again. "Remember, Tina doesn't gain anything materially by going to the police except the satisfaction of seeing you locked up. What she really wants is money and a future for Wayne. If you're in prison there's no chance of that. The police are an absolute last resort for her. You're in a better position than you think."

"Unless she sells her story to the papers. That would leave Wayne financially secure."

"We have to think positive. If we make things difficult enough for her then she might give up of her own accord." He stood up. "I'm sorry but I've got to get back to the office."

***

"Mark? Would you help me knock this stalker on the head once and for all?"

He glanced up from the evening paper. "You told me that was all sorted. If he's not giving up, you should go to the police. I'll come with you."

"But he's got a wife and family. It would wreck too many lives. I want to make myself totally unavailable and uncontactable to him. If there's absolutely no access to me that will put him off."

"You should go to the police. He's brought this on himself."

"Please, Mark. I don't want to get mixed up in a court case and be in the papers. That won't do me or him any good."

She removed his newspaper and sat down next to him. "The nightmares are probably connected to this as well. If I have to make statements and stuff it will make them worse. That will force me into the spare bedroom, which won't be much fun if we've only just got married." She placed a hand provocatively on his upper thigh.

"OK, OK. But kiss me first."

With a little more gentle persuasion Mark agreed to change his mobile number and delay distributing it widely until after the wedding. Olivia changed her number and never picked up the landline, letting it go to voicemail instead. Despite his original protests Mark didn't seem to mind his role as her temporary private chauffeur. She guessed her new dependence on him played to his inner manliness. Apart from a few calls to the landline, which Olivia ignored, Tina kept her distance and Olivia counted the days until the fairy tale safety of her marriage. Once she was Mrs Nugent it would be much harder for Tina to insist on Wayne marrying her.

But Tina still had the ammunition to make other blackmail demands in the future. There was no way around that. Olivia shuddered.

***

Tina and Wayne watched the arrivals at the church from a secluded corner of the graveyard in the shadow of a giant stone memorial. Two hundred years ago, the memorial would have been a symbol of great wealth and equally great love for the young mother who had died before her time. Now the inscription was difficult to read, the stone leaned slightly to one side and the ground around it had been colonised by dandelions. Tina stubbed a cigarette out on the stone and then dropped it into the weeds.

Wayne had told her about Olivia promising their love affair could begin as soon as she'd broken the news, gently, to Mark that their engagement was finished. To avoid ruining her brother's confidence, Tina had kept her disbelief quiet and for a couple of days Wayne had been on a high, expecting the call to come at any moment. Then Tina watched his mood deflate like a balloon with a tiny puncture. It had been obvious that Olivia would never willingly give herself to Wayne but he'd believed every word the woman had said. Tina felt like a parent trying to keep alive the Santa Claus myth, as she explained to Wayne that Olivia was probably finding it too painful to break Mark's heart and might appreciate a little helping hand from the new man in her life. After some persuasion, Wayne had agreed to come here today to give that assistance. He'd succumbed to the argument that this would be a dramatic and meaningful way of showing Olivia what she meant to him. It would show her just how much he loved and wanted her. And it would give her the chance to escape Mark and be with the man she really loved.

Few people arriving at the church would've noticed the couple, an overweight man and a skinny woman, watching and waiting in the shadows for their moment. Once she was sure everyone was inside, Tina crept to the large open wooden door and looked in. The inner glass door was closed but she could see the vicar was giving some sort of introduction. The door yielded silently to her touch and Tina walked in without anyone's head turning. She beckoned to Wayne to follow and then leaned against the stone wall at the back of the church, glad of the support. Each day she was tiring more quickly.

Tina hadn't attended many church weddings but knew her chance would come near the beginning of the service. Olivia and Mark were stood at the altar in front of the vicar. Everyone was looking at them.

"First, I am required to ask anyone present who knows a reason why these persons may not lawfully marry, to declare it now." The vicar paused for a moment and cast his eyes around the church.

There wasn't a sound. Early evening sunshine was meandering through the coloured stained glass and dust motes were dancing gently in the warm paths of light. A few people shuffled on the hard wooden seats. The vicar looked as though he was about to resume speaking.

Tina's heart thudded and she took a breath. "I have a reason," she announced and walked down the aisle towards the small group of people occupying the first few pews at the front of the church.

Everyone had turned around and she felt their eyes boring into her. There was some whispering but no one spoke out loud. Olivia appeared to be frozen to the spot, her face contorted with shock. Tina glanced behind and saw that Wayne had taken his cue and was following her.

"What's going on?" The vicar looked confused. Without his full robes he seemed to lack the authority to control events.

"I have a reason why Olivia can't get married," Tina repeated as she reached the altar.

Olivia's face was ashen and she staggered against her fiancé. Mark helped her into the empty pew at the front on the left and Tina heard him instruct her to put her head between her knees so she didn't faint.

"Olivia has been dating my brother, Wayne, and he's asked her to marry him."

"No!" Olivia's head reappeared and she stood up. "That's not true. He never asked me to marry him."

"But you *have* been dating him. That much is true. And he *will* ask you to marry him – you know that." Despite her physical frailty, Tina managed to keep her voice firm.

Olivia staggered again and sat down. There was a collective intake of breath. Mark was glancing from Olivia to Tina to Wayne and then back to his fiancée again. His mouth opened as though he was about to speak but it closed again without producing any words. Wayne grinned at everyone as though he'd won a prize and they were his appreciative audience.

The vicar found his voice and attempted to bring some order to the proceedings. "As long as Olivia and Wayne are not already married this is not a legal reason for stopping the wedding. However, if this lady's claim is true, I'm sure Olivia and Mark would appreciate some privacy now to discuss whether or not they would like the wedding to take place tomorrow as planned."

For a second there was silence and then the dozen people participating in the wedding rehearsal turned to each other and began to talk. Their voices echoed around the cavernous building in the same way reflections multiply and enlarge in a hall of mirrors. Tina watched people throw pitiful glances towards Olivia and Mark. The vicar had sat down next to the couple and was murmuring in a low voice. Tina felt like the director of a climactic scene in a soap opera.

"Go stake your claim." Tina nudged her brother. "Show that you care. Scare that posh boy Mark away. We don't want him or Olivia being persuaded that they should go ahead with the ceremony tomorrow."

"But she's upset and there's all these people watching. It's not right." The grin had faded from his face as he realised the impact their appearance had had on Olivia.

"Ladies and gentlemen." The vicar had returned to the centre aisle.

Mark was edging his way out of the pew. Once in the aisle he strode quickly to the door and left the church without once looking back. Tina watched a teenage girl jump up from the second pew and run after him. The girl glanced behind at Wayne, her face full of hate. Tina smiled. Olivia sat with her head in her hands.

"Ladies and gentlemen. Olivia and Mark have asked me to tell you that…" He paused and glanced over at Olivia and the empty space beside her, "…that there will be no wedding tomorrow."

The collective intake of breath could have been scripted.

"They would appreciate your help in contacting the other guests."

Wayne and Tina hung back as the rest of the rehearsal participants departed in a noisy buzz of conversation. Some of them pointed, whispered or stared openly as they passed Wayne.

"He's just *so* not Olivia's type."

"How could she choose him over Mark?"

"It's so totally unbelievable. I didn't have Olivia down as the unfaithful kind."

Tina could feel her brother wilting beside her at all the negative comments. "Take no notice," she whispered. "They're just people with more money than sense. You're worth a thousand of them any day. Remember – today Olivia has chosen you over Mark. That proves her love for you." From the corner of her eye she saw Wayne's ample chest puff out a little bit.

Joanne had moved forward a row to sit next to Olivia. She had her arm around her friend's shoulders.

"Time to move in for the kill. Go and stake your claim." Tina gave Wayne a little push and he walked slowly over to the front left pew, casting a glance back at Tina every few steps.

Olivia looked up as he approached and she said something to Joanne who got up and left the church, a doubtful expression on her face. The vicar was hovering, pretending to tidy the hymn books and he looked disapproving as Wayne squeezed his bulk into the pew. Tina couldn't hear what was said. Olivia didn't turn her head, she kept it bowed and shook it from side to side. It was a negative, defeatist gesture. The vicar disappeared through a door marked, 'Vestry'.

"Well?" Tina demanded when Wayne returned without Olivia.

"She's a broken woman and it's my fault."

"Rubbish. She brought this on herself by her actions as a teenager. She was a tough cookie back then and people don't change that much. Give her a couple of days and she'll bounce back and find a way to make life with you work. A life of freedom with you is better than a life in prison."

"But she doesn't love me. She loves Mark."

"That doesn't matter." Tina pulled Wayne into the nearest pew. "You know I haven't got much time left. I promised our mum I'd always look after you. Once I'm dead I can't do that."

Wayne sniffed and blew his nose. He pulled the photo of their mother out of his pocket.

"But Olivia *can* look after you, financially at least. This isn't about the love between you and Olivia. It's about the love that Mum felt for you when she made me promise to look after you. It's about the love that Simon's mum felt for me in prison when she promised that Simon and Olivia would always help us on the outside. It's about the love I feel for you. Because I love you, I want to make sure you're taken care of when I'm gone. There's lots of love in this tangled web so don't worry if it's missing between you and Olivia at first."

Olivia walked past their pew without a sideways glance. She held her head high.

"Give 'er a couple of days and she'll be as right as rain. Hard as nails she is."

"But we don't have the proof to send her to prison anymore. The paper's gone and that's my fault, isn't it? And I don't want her to be locked up, she doesn't deserve it."

"She thinks we have the proof and that's a good enough threat to hold over her."

There was a thud as the vicar came back through the vestry door and let it slam shut behind him. He had a large key in his hand and paused alongside the pew where Wayne and Tina were sitting. "I need to lock up."

Tina pushed herself up to standing. The pain in her back had worsened. It was a week until her next check-up and she knew the prognosis wouldn't be good.

20

Olivia hadn't been to bed. She'd sat in the kitchen all night hoping Mark would turn up or at least call. He'd done neither. She was scared to ring him. She would break into one hundred pieces if she had to hear him reject her again. Her face still burned at the humiliation she'd felt when he'd spoken to the vicar as though she wasn't there.

"Incredible though it is, I believe *him*," he'd said, indicating Wayne in the aisle. "There's no smoke without fire. She's had a couple of thinly explained nights out. She even invented a stalker to cover her tracks. There's been nightmares and talk of moving into the spare room. She's been acting abnormally for a few weeks. Now it all makes sense."

Olivia had said nothing. She couldn't tell the truth and her brain wouldn't work quickly enough to give any other explanation for the presence of Tina and Wayne.

"She isn't denying it now," Mark had continued. "I can't marry her tomorrow with this huge doubt in my mind."

Her fiancé hadn't even said goodbye to her or that he was sorry it had to end like that. He'd simply got up and marched out of the church.

Outside the kitchen window a new day was beginning. The

sun was shining, birds were singing, traffic noise was building. Life was going on as normal. In the house, despite the ticking clock, time had stood still. Nothing good would ever happen again. For a second Olivia's sleep-starved brain didn't register that the doorbell had rung. When it rang a second time she jumped up. Mark! The figure behind the glass was the right height. Her heart pounded, she had to say or do something to make him love her again. She opened the door.

It was Joanne. She was holding a small gift basket of fruit wrapped in cellophane and embellished with a large red bow.

"Oh."

"I'm sorry. Flowers didn't seem appropriate but I wanted to bring you something."

"What for?"

"Last night in the church, I left you with that man. I'm not sure it was the right thing for a best friend to do. The truth is last night I still hadn't forgiven you for trying to split up Simon and me. I didn't know whether I wanted to be your best friend or any sort of friend at all."

"Oh."

"But you've obviously got weird pressures in your life right now. I guess your stupid comments about Simon being unfaithful to me were due to whatever you've got going on. No lasting harm was done so let's be friends again."

"Yes, please!" Olivia hugged her friend. Right now, a best friend was the thing she needed most in the world – apart from Mark agreeing to take her back.

"That man in the church didn't look at all your type." Joanne put the basket of fruit on the kitchen work surface.

"No." The size of the lump in her throat made it hard to talk.

"Are you OK?"

"No." Olivia started to cry. The tears came from nowhere and the sobs caused her to almost double over. All night she'd kept this emotion in check but one kind thought from a friend had opened the flood gates. Joanne gave her another hug and after a couple of minutes Olivia managed to compose herself.

"Is this linked to how you were at the hen night?" Joanne asked. "You were definitely afraid of something then. I rang Mark the next morning to find out how you were. He said you hadn't mentioned being taken ill. Part of this fiasco might be my fault. If I hadn't aroused his suspicions that you were hiding something, he might have gone ahead with the wedding. I'm so sorry, Olivia."

"It's not your fault. I've given him plenty of reasons to doubt me – nightmares, a stalker, unscheduled nights out." Olivia mumbled into a tissue her friend had produced. Joanne's arms embraced her again. Her voice was calm but incomprehensible through Olivia's veil of misery. Gentle arms guided her onto a kitchen chair. A wodge of kitchen roll was put in her hand. She heard water pounding into the kettle followed by the click of a switch and the building crescendo of the water coming up to the boil. She blew her nose several times, took a deep breath and opened her eyes. They felt narrow and puffy. Joanne was rifling through cupboards.

"Mugs to your left and teabags to your right." Olivia managed.

"Sugar?"

"Don't take it."

"You need it. I bet you haven't had any breakfast?"

Olivia shook her head. The thought of food hadn't appealed earlier but now she remembered she'd eaten nothing since the previous lunchtime. "A piece of toast would be nice."

Ten minutes later there were two mugs of hot sweet tea between them, a plate of buttered toast and a jar of marmalade.

"I've come to help," said Joanne. "When all the toast's gone, give me a list and we'll start."

"Help? You think we can get Mark to—" For a moment her spirits soared.

"No. I spoke to Mark first thing this morning. He says when

things have settled down you can explain properly to him in person, maybe then there might be hope. But he can't marry you today. I think he's got too many doubts buzzing around in his head and the humiliation of last night finished him off."

Olivia concentrated on chewing the piece of toast in her mouth. It had turned into tasteless cardboard. Her humiliation was much worse than Mark's. She was cast as the baddy in all of this. "Aren't you going to ask me what this is about? Aren't you going to ask me who those two people were that burst into the church?"

"No. You'll tell me when the time is right. This morning we need to go through your lists and cancel everything. And quickly!"

"I can't. I can't tell people my wedding is cancelled."

"It has to be done or there'll be flowers and a hairdresser turning up here shortly. If you can't do it, I will."

Olivia listened as Joanne made endless calls unpicking all the arrangements that had taken months to put in place. She also phoned all the guests, cutting each one short as they started to express how sorry they were and moving onto the next. Olivia remained at the kitchen table.

"All done! And my throat's as dry as sandpaper. More tea?"

Joanne left at lunchtime. Olivia felt slightly better for the moral support, tea and toast. Joanne hadn't asked a single question about Wayne which had made things easier, other people wouldn't be so tactful. Olivia had to deal with him and Tina once and for all. She couldn't let them steal her future like this.

At 2pm instead of walking down the aisle, she was walking down a garden path. Instead of greeting her husband-to-be at the altar she was giving a rueful smile to her ex-husband as he answered her knock. Instead of Wagner played on the church organ there was the background chatter of a sports pundit on Five Live.

Simon held her close without speaking. "Joanne called me last night and told me what happened," he said finally. "This is my fault – if only my mum hadn't met that wretched woman in prison and made that stupid promise about us helping Tina and Wayne. If only she hadn't joined that creative writing class or written down our names in that letter."

"Don't forget I'm the reason why your mum went to prison. Your mum is the innocent party here. I'm the guilty one." She paused. "Simon, I need concrete help to get Tina and Wayne out of my life. For good. I want Mark back."

"I'm with you there – I can't make more excuses for Wayne at work. He has to go. But I can't put Joanne at risk from Tina again by sacking him."

"I swear, no matter what Tina threatens, I will not even consider hurting Joanne again on her behalf. She is a fabulous friend and I don't deserve her." Olivia had decided she would do nothing more that would compromise her own morals or hurt those close to her – whatever the cost to her personally.

"So we either destroy Tina and Wayne or we destroy the proof that she's dangling over you," Simon said. "I've been thinking about this since Joanne called last night. I think I have a workable plan."

***

It was early evening when Olivia got back home. Through the glass in the front door she could see the kitchen light was on. Mark was back! In her haste to get to him she fumbled her key and it seemed to take forever to get it in the lock the right way up.

"Mark!" She didn't bother removing shoes or coat.

"It's not Dad, it's me." Suzanne appeared in the kitchen doorway. "He doesn't know I'm here."

"Oh." The disappointment was like a soaking of cold water. "How is he?"

"I stayed at his house last night. It didn't seem right to leave him and go home to Mum's. But I don't think he went to bed. This morning he was wearing exactly the same clothes as last night and there wasn't a wet towel in the bathroom so he hadn't had a shower."

"Has he said anything?"

"He just keeps saying that he can't believe you would do this to him. He says he was looking forward to growing old with you and now it will never happen."

Olivia blinked hard and put her hand to her mouth. "We used to joke how we'd turn into two old biddies in rocking chairs with a cat on the hearth rug."

"What happened, Olivia? Why did you choose that oaf rather than my dad? I wanted you to be my step-mum. You're the best person that Dad has ever dated."

The teenager was looking at her with confusion and tears in her eyes. The poor thing had already been through the trauma of her parents getting divorced and now she'd got this upheaval as well. Olivia felt she owed Suzanne an explanation.

"It wasn't as simple as choosing one person rather than another. There were… certain lifestyle choices I also had to take into account. There was no real choice – it was thrust upon me."

Suzanne's expression told her she'd muddied the waters rather than clarified anything.

"Was it… I saw your car… on the estate."

"You were on the estate?" Olivia was shocked.

Suzanne nodded. "That boy…"

"The one your dad didn't want at the evening do?"

Another nod. "He lives on the estate. We were with his mates and I saw you pick up the fat man and then, later, come back and go in the flats. Your car was still there when I came home."

Olivia remembered the lads. Suzanne shouldn't be mixing with them. Now, in her mind's eye, she could see the vulnerable-looking girl with the hoodie pulled right up. Her mind switched away from her own problems. "Are you in love with him?"

"Sort of." Suzanne looked uncomfortable. "When he's on his own. He's angry the wedding's off – he'd bought new clothes."

"You didn't univite him after what your dad said?"

"No – it would've made me look stupid. He might have finished with me."

"Oh, Suzanne." Olivia hugged her. "Being worried about looking stupid is no foundation for a relationship."

"But he liked me, he called me his girlfriend. He didn't notice my cushion tummy like the girls at school do." She prodded her middle. "And every day, without fail, he was outside the college. Not like Mum, sometimes she's at home and sometimes she's not. And Dad's got you. At least with Dean, I've got someone too."

There were tears in Olivia's eyes again but this time they were on Suzanne's behalf. "Is this why you were having second thoughts about university?"

"I don't want to lose him, Olivia. I don't want to lose him like you've lost Dad. But I want him to be nice to me all the time. I don't want to be paraded like a prize cow in front of his mates." Then Suzanne cried.

Olivia was grateful for the distraction of someone else's problem and also for the fact her almost-step-daughter hadn't pursued any further explanation about the fat man.

"I came round to bring your house key back." Suzanne had pulled herself together and was taking a silver key off a large keyring with a koala bear attached. "If Dad's not welcome then I guess I'm not either."

"You are both welcome anytime. Keep the key. Please. And come any time you want."

"Do you mean it?" Suzanne looked genuinely grateful.

21

"You do know what day it is today?" Olivia asked as soon as she picked up Simon's call. There was a slight catch in her voice. "I didn't calculate what the date would be when you suggested next Saturday otherwise I'd have changed it."

"This isn't the time for riddles, Olivia. Everything's set for this evening and we need to coordinate our actions. The plan starts in a few minutes."

"It's our son's birthday. He was born innocent and he died innocent, after a life that was much too short. I don't want the date of his birth sullied."

A wave of guilt hit Simon. He hadn't realised today was David's birthday. Did that make him a bad dad? Why hadn't Olivia said so before? Neither of them could afford to be emotional tonight. Feelings and sensitivities had to stay out of it.

"Everything's in place," he said in a firm voice. "We have to go ahead now, regardless of the day. I'm sorry."

"I just wanted you to know the date was special."

"OK. But let's focus on the present."

He heard the faint sound of a doorbell.

"I think they're here." She spoke more quietly. "I told them 7 pm and it's two minutes to. I'll text like we planned."

Five minutes later Simon got the message confirming Tina and Wayne had arrived at Olivia's house for dinner. The coast was clear for him to retrieve the evidence of Olivia's guilt from their flat. He parked half a mile from the estate and, despite the warmth of the evening, kept the hood of his sweatshirt up. He didn't want anybody able to describe him or his car. There were gloves stuffed in his rucksack but he didn't want to attract attention on a warm evening by wearing them until it was absolutely necessary. He chose to walk up the steps to the seventh floor, thinking he'd meet fewer people than if he took the lift.

There was a sour smell in the stairwell, chewing gum stuck to the walls, and empty cans left on windowsills and in corners. On the seventh floor landing a door opened and an elderly man came out with an equally elderly spaniel on a lead. They both moved very slowly and the man spent a long time putting his door key away in a purse which he dropped into a large shopping bag. To avoid loitering suspiciously, Simon was forced to continue up to the eighth floor while the man and his dog waited for the lift.

Five minutes later the landing was deserted and Simon examined the flat door. His only experience of breaking and entering was from the TV. This door had a pane of frosted glass almost filling the top third of the door. It would require a hammer. He extracted hammer and gloves from his bag, keeping an eye on the stairwell, lift and the other doors around him. It took two swift blows to make a big enough hole in the bottom right of the pane to get his hand through. He winced at the noise but television sets were shouting through the neighbouring doors and nobody stirred. Despite the thick gloves and the sleeve of his sweatshirt, his skin still got nicked as he reached through to release the Yale lock.

He kicked as much of the broken glass inside the flat as he could and closed the door behind him. The hallway was dim, lit only by the light seeping in from the half-open door to the lounge and the yellow strip light on the landing which sent illumination through the broken window. Simon had already decided that the important piece of paper would be somewhere in Tina's bedroom. It would not have been entrusted to Wayne and nor would it be somewhere that a casual visitor might stumble across it. He opened a door and discovered Wayne's room. A pair of jeans and a T-shirt were on a hanger over the outside of the wardrobe door. They were damp to the touch and had been left to dry neatly after a wash. Three pairs of trainers were lined up against the wall, each with the laces tucked inside. On the bedside table was an adult magazine beneath a box of tissues. The curtains were open and a pleasant draught came in through one of the windows.

Simon found the bathroom door next and moved straight on. The bedroom adjacent to the lounge was obviously female. The pink floral curtains were tied back and there was a breeze in here too. The bed was made. Simon walked in. He still wore the gloves. There were three fading photos on the dressing-table. They showed a much younger Tina and Wayne with another, older, woman, possibly their mother. A half-full glass of water sat on the bedside cabinet alongside three boxes of tablets each with a white label indicating which pharmacy they'd been dispensed from and the dosage instructions.

He opened the cupboard of the cabinet. It contained a pile of papers and a paperback novel with yellowing pages and a charity shop price sticker. The papers excited Simon – this was easier than he'd expected. He started leafing through them, looking for anything handwritten. There were plenty of typed letters but they were mostly hospital appointments. They mentioned consultants, oncology and radiotherapy. Despite his hatred of her, Simon felt a pang of sadness for Tina. Maybe the cancer and associated medication were clouding her judgement and making her do things no ordinary person would. He carefully placed the medical paperwork and book back in the small cupboard.

The wardrobe was worth a look. When he was little, his mother had had an old Quality Street tin on the top shelf of the wardrobe. It was where she kept special birthday cards, photographs and anything that Simon had made for her. He had no idea what happened to the tin after she was jailed and the house was sold. There were footsteps on the concrete landing. He stiffened.

"Look at that."

"Bloody vandals."

The voices were slightly muffled. They came from outside the front door. Simon's heart thudded. He didn't dare move.

"Do you think it's a break in?"

"Tina did say they were going out tonight. I'll text her and let her know. It's not fair, her having the cancer as well. She's not 'ad a lot of luck in her life."

"There it's sent. Are you coming in for a cuppa?"

Simon heard the sound of a door open and close. He let out the breath he hadn't realised he was holding. Now Tina might reappear at any minute. He began quickly shifting the clothes in the wardrobe to one side.

***

Tina's handbag beeped.

"You've got a text," said Wayne. "I'll get it for you."

"No. Just pass me the bag."

"More potatoes?" asked Olivia, her voice full of false brightness.

"Yeah," said Wayne. "Roast potatoes are my favourite."

"Not for me." Tina was fiddling with her phone. "I can't manage big meals now. I have trouble keeping 'em down."

Tina was pale, too thin and often shifted her position,

seeming in discomfort on the high-backed dining chair. But Olivia wasn't going to ask about her health, she didn't want to feign sympathy.

"We've had a break-in." Tina looked up from the phone, her eyes wide and shock imprinted on her pinched face. "Julie from across the landing says the front door glass is broken. We better go 'ome. I'll call us a taxi."

"Oh no! Please don't go." Olivia had no idea whether Simon had found the vital piece of paper or whether he was still inside the flat. A taxi would take a maximum of fifteen minutes to get Tina and Wayne home. Olivia put on her most pleasant smile and leaned towards Wayne, who was sitting next to her. She stroked the repulsive flab on his upper arm where the short sleeve of his shirt finished. "It's really good having this chance to get to know each other properly seeing as we'll soon be family. And we haven't had dessert yet. I've done homemade treacle pudding and custard."

"I love custard," said Wayne. "Can I pour my own from the jug?"

"Absolutely."

"The flat might be trashed." Tina looked torn.

"The damage is already done," said Olivia. "Whether you go home now or in a couple of hours the result will be the same. The thugs will be long gone. Let's finish the meal and then I'll drive you home, go in with you and help you sort things out. Isn't that what family and friends are for?"

"But it's our 'ome. They might be trashing it inside."

"It'll be OK, Tina. Olivia's got the best idea. Let's all go together when we've finished the meal. If we need to call the police, Olivia will be better at dealing with that than us."

Olivia suppressed a sigh of relief, Wayne might not always be the sharpest knife in the drawer but he could talk sense sometimes. She took the plates from the main course into the kitchen and texted Simon. 'You've been spotted. I can only keep them here another hour.'

"Let's set a date for the wedding," said Tina when Olivia took the pudding in. "Shall we say the first Saturday in August?"

The question took Olivia by surprise. She touched Wayne's arm again, trying to slip into the role of someone who really wanted to marry this oaf. "I need longer than that – after all the upset of last weekend. Can't Wayne and I decide at our leisure?"

As Tina's mouth opened to argue, there was a beep from the kitchen.

Olivia jumped up. "Must have left the microwave on."

In the kitchen her phone was flashing. 'Looked everywhere. Found nothing. Can you search her handbag?'

Olivia cursed under her breath. She'd seen Tina put the bag on the floor after she'd retrieved her beeping phone. Tina's chair was near the door into the hallway. Bending down and picking the bag up would be too obvious. The alternative was to dribble the bag to the door with her foot. She went back into the dining room.

"That was lovely." Wayne sat back in his chair. "Just as good as when Mum used to get those sponge puddings in tins as a Sunday treat."

"More custard?" Olivia passed the jug over to him without waiting for a reply.

Wayne poured himself another bowlful and sucked each mouthful off the spoon with a slurping noise. "Me and Tina will wash up for you," he offered when the last of the thick yellow sludge had been scraped from the dish.

"There's no need. I've got a dishwasher."

"We can load it for you." Wayne got to his feet. "I know how to do it. Me mate's bird's got a dishwasher."

Fearing for her china and glassware, Olivia was about to protest. Then she changed her mind – it would get them out of the way whilst she delved into Tina's handbag. "That would be kind. Thank you. I'll do some tidying away in here."

Olivia gritted her teeth and ignored the sound of clinking

plates and glasses. Broken china didn't matter if she could get these two half-wits out of her life. Heart thumping, bent over and half-hidden by the folds of the tablecloth, she unzipped the handbag and ran her hand through the contents. It was standard female paraphernalia, tissues, purse, comb, pen, keys and a few receipts. No letters. She checked for zipped compartments. Her hopes leapt when she found a zip in the side of the bag. It contained only a collection of lottery tickets.

There was a beep from the kitchen again. Olivia smacked her head against the edge of the table as she tried to stand up quickly. For a second she saw stars.

"What you doing with my bag? And there's a message on your phone from Simon." Tina was standing in the kitchen doorway holding Olivia's phone. Her voice was hard and her eyes distrustful. "He says: Searched everywhere. Nothing found. Think she's fabricated the evidence & it's OK to call their bluff. Let them go. Call me later."

Tina put the phone down behind her on the kitchen worktop. Olivia was silent. Her head was throbbing from its smash against the table and she couldn't think straight.

"I don't like people who break into my flat. And there was no evidence to find because it's somewhere else for safekeeping. It does exist. Do I look like a liar?"

Olivia said nothing.

Wayne was frowning. "It's not nice to break into the flat of the person you're going to marry. Do you really love me or were you lying to me about the love affair?"

Still, there was nothing Olivia could say.

"Fetch the carving knife, Wayne. I've seen it on the draining board." Tina's voice was as sharp as a blade.

Wayne didn't move. The friendly vibes he'd been giving off all evening had suddenly changed. Olivia could feel, as well as see by the way he was staring at her, he was a man suddenly scorned. In the last sixty seconds he'd realised there was never going to be a love affair. She felt threatened, more threatened than when he'd pointed the penknife at her throat in his bungled kidnap attempt.

"Does this mean," he said carefully, "that you don't want to marry me?" His face showed the great big penny had just dropped. Olivia's kind words to him had been lies. "You never wanted to have a love affair with me, did you?"

"You've got this wrong, Wayne, love." Olivia tried to force a passable note of kindness into her voice. "Simon was the one who wanted to break into your flat, not me. He was angry about Joanne getting hurt. Stupidly I admitted that was my doing and then I had tell him the whole story. I had to tell him why I hurt Joanne. I told him about the evidence Tina says she has. It was his idea to steal it, so he could protect Joanne. Really – I didn't want to be part of his plan."

"I don't just *say* I have the evidence. I *do* have it. Fetch the carving knife, Wayne. And lock the back door and bring me the key."

This time Wayne hesitated only to throw Olivia a look of pure hatred. She felt like she'd been punched. He returned with the long sharp blade and Olivia realised she was trembling. She gripped the back of a dining chair with both hands. She didn't want Tina to see how scared she was. Her knuckles went white with the effort of keeping her hands and arms still.

"The key, Wayne?"

Wayne handed it over and Tina slipped it into the pocket of her trousers. Then she made Wayne stand at the doorway from the dining room into the hall, barring any escape route. Wayne raised the knife and adopted the aggressive pose of a Samurai warrior.

For several minutes the three of them stood in silence. Tina's malevolent eyes didn't move from Olivia. The hate in her gaze was intense. A small smile of enjoyment played on Wayne's mouth. Occasionally he contorted his lips, raised the arm holding the knife higher and narrowed his eyes, mimicking Tina's expression of dislike.

"Tina, I'm confused," Olivia ventured. "Why are you holding me hostage?"

"You know very well."

"No, I don't. You've been lying. You have no evidence against me. You have no hold over me. I'd like you both to leave my house. Please."

Wayne glanced at his sister. The arm holding the knife drooped a little.

"Now, Wayne! Her neck!"

Suddenly the fleshy arm had her in a neck-hold and the knife had drawn blood on her throat. She felt a dribble of liquid run over her skin and nestle at her collar bone where her locket sat.

"Watch your step." Tina's words ricocheted like bullets. "I hold all the power. That evidence does exist but I wasn't stupid enough to leave it in the flat for any Tom, Dick or Simon to find. It's safely locked away in a bank vault."

"You mean in those rows of little boxes? Like on the telly?" Wayne relaxed his neck-hold a fraction. "But I thought it was—"

"I mean exactly like that." Tina's eyes never left Olivia.

"Wow! That's like *Hustle* come to life. I didn't know ordinary people could use those." Wayne spoke excitedly. "So you don't have to be rich then?"

"No, you don't have to be rich. But that brings us to the heart of our trouble here." She nodded to Wayne and Olivia grunted as his hold around her neck tightened again. "Some people have more money than is good for them and others have very little…"

Wayne's stranglehold was forcing Olivia to concentrate hard on her breathing and on remaining calm, but another thought niggled at the back of her mind. The mention of safety deposit boxes had reminded her of something she couldn't quickly put her finger on.

"Equality is what they're always talking about on the news. Me and Wayne are going to make sure we get our fair share from you. That evidence in the bank box will make sure you give it to us. As your husband, Wayne will be entitled to half of everything you have. Equal shares, that's fair."

Olivia concentrated on the past. Mark's mum had a safe under the stairs containing her jewellery. "So, why the knife?" Her voice came out as a croak because of the pressure on her windpipe.

"To make sure you get the message that I mean business." That nod at Wayne again and this time Tina raised her hand to head height and brought it across her own throat in a cutting motion.

Olivia closed her eyes and waited. He gave her only another little nick. Which was worse, a slow death by a thousand cuts or incarceration for a crime she committed three decades ago? "OK. You've made your point. I know you're serious. What do you want me to do? Why don't we talk about this wedding that you want in a civilised manner, without the knife?"

"I want you to suffer. Suffer like Audrey did in prison. At the start she was the victim of every bully around. I saved her. But when I was gone it all started again. She couldn't cope and so she topped herself. You deserve to suffer and feel the fear like she did."

Olivia blinked rapidly to stop the tears. Her lifelong guilt about Audrey plus the immediate terror of losing her own life was making it impossible to stay calm. A sob rose in her chest but it couldn't get past Wayne's neck-hold and it went back down with a gulp of air.

"You're going to suffer like I did when the stress of being locked up with all those low-life women killed my unborn baby." Another nod at Wayne and another nick on her neck.

My baby died too! But Olivia said nothing. Talking about David on his birthday with this mad woman would sully his memory. She closed her eyes and pictured his chubby, kicking legs, the smile he mastered only a week before his death and his smell. Did all babies have such a unique smell or did David have it because he was special?

"You're going to suffer like my mum did when she died in pain." Tina had come up close now and pushed her face into Olivia's. Her breath smelt sour and there was body odour too, not quite masked by the cheap perfume that clung to Tina's clothes. "She died not knowing what would become of her only son."

The bank deposit boxes, something didn't make sense. Mark's mother had shown her the jewellery in the safe. Most of it was heirlooms, like the sapphire engagement ring belonging to a grandmother and a gold bracelet adorned with a lifetime's collection of charms. There were also a couple of more modern pieces in platinum and white gold which Mark's father had bought in recent years for his wife.

"I wanted you to see it all," Mark's mother had said, "because in my will I shall split it between you and Suzanne. You make Mark very happy and after… his first marriage… that makes me very glad."

"You're going to suffer like I am now." Tina's bony finger repeatedly struck Olivia's chest to make the point. "I'm fighting terminal cancer AND trying to keep a promise I made to my dying mum. I promised I would make a good future for Wayne, her son, my brother. That's difficult in a world where no one cares about those less clever than themselves."

Tina stepped away. She pulled a dining chair towards her and sat down a few feet from Olivia. Exhaustion showed in the greyness of her skin, the deep grooves around her eyes and the small lines radiating from the creased red paint of her mouth. It was impossible not to feel some pity for the woman.

"Can't the authorities help?" Olivia croaked. "Mental health's quite a hot issue at the moment."

"So you want to make Wayne suffer, too? By locking him

up in a looney-bin?" Tina's glare was contemptuous. "No way. Wayne's as gentle as a lamb. The psychos in those places would make mincemeat out of him."

Tina talked like a woman slowly losing her grip on the world. In one breath she strung together articulate sentences about suffering but then, in the next, she made totally unfounded statements about how she guessed mentally unwell patients might be treated.

The clock was the only sound now. Olivia closed her eyes, wanting to transport herself to a better place. One of the white gold pieces of jewellery had particularly appealed to her. It was a bangle with two embedded diamonds. Mark's mother had let her try it on. It was easy to wear and would go with just about anything – dressy or casual. She'd asked Mark's mother if they were worried about burglars with all these valuable pieces in the house.

Olivia opened her eyes with a start. That niggle at the back of her mind – she knew what it was! Mark's mother had said they used to keep the bulk of the jewellery collection in a safety deposit box at the bank but a couple of years previously the bank had stopped offering the service. They'd enquired elsewhere but those boxes were a service that was gradually being withdrawn by all banks. Mark's father had been reluctant to switch to a private provider so they'd installed the safe under the stairs instead.

"Which bank is holding the evidence for you?" She kept the excitement from her voice.

Tina looked taken aback and she paused just a little too long. "Barclays. Why? Do you think your mate Simon can break into banks as well as the flats of vulnerable women?"

"I just wondered." Olivia managed not to smile. Knowing for sure Tina had no evidence against her provided a few moments of relief and then the knife at her throat nicked again when Tina inclined her head to give another signal to Wayne.

22

Now it was completely dark outside. The dining-room clock was behind her and Wayne's grip meant Olivia couldn't manoeuvre her arm to see her watch. She guessed it was at least 11pm. The lights were on but the curtains were still open. If someone walked past, the three of them would be actors in the spotlight – on show but unable to see into the darkness of the auditorium. However, the dining-room and kitchen were at the back of the house so any passer-by was unlikely. Olivia's neck was aching from being held in Wayne's stranglehold. He had abandoned his warrior pose and the knife hung from his free hand. Tina grimaced from time to time and shifted on her seat, as though she was in pain.

The table hadn't been fully cleared after the meal. The salt and pepper and the cream jug were still in the centre along with the vase containing the carnations Olivia had bought at the supermarket. Three crumpled napkins marked the places where the three of them had sat. Wayne's was obvious from the sticky yellow mark where he'd wiped his lips after the second helping of custard. When this was all over those napkins and the table cloth would be burnt. She didn't want to live with the memories of this night. It would be impossible to continue living here at all. The house would have to be sold and she'd buy something quite different. Perhaps she'd move somewhere far away. If Mark didn't want her, there was no reason to stay. An ambulance wailed in the distance.

A thump on the window made them all jump. Tina looked panicked and started to lever herself up from the chair.

"A bat," Olivia said. "We get them crashing into the glass occasionally."

Tina relaxed again. The line of tension across Olivia's shoulder blades remained. She clenched and unclenched her fists. The audible tick from the clock seemed to have slowed to a crawl. A fox had the audacity to stare in through the patio glass. The old lady next door fed it scraps every night and it had become unnaturally brave around humans.

"I need the toilet, Tina." Wayne shuffled his feet behind Olivia.

Tina sighed and shook her head as though he was a small boy who'd refused to go when told and was now suffering the consequences. "Can't you wait?"

Olivia tried to turn her head to look at her captor but his neck-hold made it impossible.

"No, it's urgent."

"There's one at the bottom of the stairs," Olivia said "First door on your left from the front door." This was surreal. She sounded as though she was talking to an ordinary guest in her home and not an unstable man wielding a carving knife.

"Give me the knife before you let go of her neck." It took a few seconds for Tina to get up from the chair.

Olivia ended up against the dining room wall with Tina pointing the knife at her chest. The sick woman didn't have the strength to mimic her brother's neck hold. Wayne scurried into the hallway and the bolt on the toilet door shot home. In the quiet they could hear him relieving himself.

"What's the point of this?" Olivia asked. "How long are you going to hold me here?"

"Until you've suffered enough. And that will be a long, long time."

The taps turned on and off several times before Wayne came back and they all took up their previous positions. Olivia concentrated on breathing deeply and slowly. It was important she kept her wits about her. The fox looked in again on its way back from next door. This time it had something indistinguishable but dead hanging from its mouth.

Then Olivia's bladder could take it no longer and she had to suffer the embarrassment of squeezing into the downstairs toilet with Tina, the knife at her throat or chest the whole time.

"This is nowhere near the humiliation that Audrey suffered in prison," Tina said when Olivia complained.

Back in the dining-room, the clock said 3:20 am. Tina brought up the subject of Wayne and Olivia's wedding again. She talked about having it mid-week so they could get a date much sooner. Wayne said he'd already asked his mate to be best man and apparently Tina knew a young girl on the estate, granddaughter of a friend, who was dying to be a bridesmaid.

"You've already got your dress, so we could get it all arranged with a hotel wedding planner tomorrow. It shouldn't take too long to get a dress made up for little Katie. A quiet do at a posh hotel – that should be within your budget, Olivia. After we've booked it, the three of us could have a posh afternoon tea to celebrate – a sort of engagement party."

"If you like." There was nothing to be gained by not playing along.

Then they were each lost in their own thoughts again. It was almost silent. Traffic noise had reduced to only the odd vehicle and even the wildlife appeared to have retired for the night. Olivia's legs and back were aching.

"Could Wayne and I sit down, please? He can sit facing me with the knife at my throat. But at least let us rest our legs."

"No. You stay standing and you stay awake – all night. This

is about suffering. Afterwards it will make you grateful for what you've got."

***

Suzanne woke early. It was another sunny day and the thin curtains in her room at her dad's offered little protection against the brightness. She pulled the quilt over her head to shut out the light. It was Sunday, she didn't have to get up. But the heat beneath the quilt was stifling and, in order to breathe, she was forced to push it back and accept that she wouldn't be going back to sleep. Reluctantly her brain made the transition from night to day. There was homework to be done and the personal statement to be drafted for her UCAS form. And there was Dad to deal with.

After talking to Olivia the previous week she'd tried to make a logical decision about whether to continue seeing Dean. She'd written a list and the good bits of having him outweighed the bad. So they were still together. He'd suggested that she chuck school seeing as she wasn't going to university.

"I can't leave without a college course lined up," she'd said and it was the truth. "Plus A' levels will help with whatever I do next." She hadn't told him that the teachers at school had more or less insisted she apply to university. They'd explained that by doing this she wasn't closing any other doors because she could change her mind at any time. That had been a relief – it meant she had another twelve months to decide if Dean was who she really wanted to be with. She was worried she didn't properly love him – no one has to write a list of the good and bad points of someone they truly love.

The problem of Dad couldn't be solved with a list. He hadn't been to work in the week since the wedding rehearsal. His boss had been on the guest list and therefore what had happened would be all around the office. Dad had said he couldn't face the whispering and finger-pointing.

190

"I had a week's holiday booked for the honeymoon anyway – so I'm not letting anyone down."

"But you'll go back on Monday?"

"Probably not. There doesn't seem much point in doing anything anymore." He'd rubbed his forehead as though he had a headache. Suzanne noticed the crows' feet around his eyes had deepened. His skin was pale from lack of both sleep and sunlight.

"But, Dad, the longer you leave it, the harder it will be."

Her father had just shrugged. Earlier in the week Suzanne had called round every day after school to check he was OK. When it became obvious he wasn't eating, hardly sleeping and not washing, she started staying over. But still he refused to go out into the world. At first Suzanne brought the necessities of life in and then she stopped, in the hope of forcing him out. Eventually he'd gone to the supermarket – at 1 am.

"Why, Dad? Why in the middle of the night?"

"Because no one I know shops at that time of day."

There was no answer to that and Suzanne had tried a different tack. "I think you should go and see Olivia. From what she told me, it's not just a case of her preferring that fat oaf to you. There's more to it but she wouldn't tell me. She might talk to you."

"No, Suzanne, the writing was on the wall for our relationship and I should have noticed it a long time ago. I'm not going to humiliate myself any further by going round there. Olivia's been keeping secrets from me. It started with the nightmares, then she invented a stalker and made me protect her, she hypothesised about paying money to an unspecified person on a regular basis, she didn't tell me about being taken ill on her hen night and conveniently forgot to tell me about another night out she had planned."

"But—"

Her father had interrupted her by holding up his hand like

a traffic policeman. "I was stupid. All the way along the line I made excuses for her."

Now the birds were proclaiming their enjoyment of the sunshine through choral singing. Suzanne got out of bed and went to the bathroom. Her father's bedroom door was still shut. She deliberately made a bucketful of noise in the shower and then clattered downstairs and banged cupboard doors as she made coffee and got cereal. Her dad needed to get up but she wanted him to do it of his own accord, rather than after she banged on his door.

Fifteen minutes later he made an appearance in a T-shirt and short pyjama bottoms. From across the room she heard the growl from his stomach. That's what came of having an appetite for only a quarter of the lasagne she'd cooked him the night before. He headed towards the cupboard behind her but she held up her hand and shook her head.

"No cereal until you're washed and dressed."

His eyes went to the coffee pot.

"And no coffee." She held his favourite mug hostage in her right fist.

"You win." He padded slowly from the room like an old man.

He reappeared a few minutes later in yesterday's shirt and jeans. She frowned.

"No clothes left." He held up both hands in a defeatist shrug.

"As soon as you've eaten, we're going to Olivia's to collect your stuff." Over the last few days their parent/child roles had been reversed but she was going to bully him back into being a responsible father. Suzanne didn't want to be the strong one in their relationship; she wanted her dad back and she wanted Olivia too. She loved Olivia almost as much as she loved her dad. She wasn't a mother replacement she was the big sister that Suzanne had never had. She was the best friend that had never materialised from Suzanne's school acquaintances and losing her so suddenly and inexplicably was hard. Despite what had happened Olivia said she wanted her and Suzanne still to be friends but going round there on her own felt like a betrayal to Dad and Suzanne couldn't do it. This breakup wasn't as life-exploding as her parents' divorce but it was a medium quake in the foundations of her life. She'd been five when her parents separated and powerless to do anything about it. Now she was almost seventeen, and beginning to understand that if you wanted something you had to fight for it – otherwise life drifted by leaving nothing in its wake but regrets. She didn't want to regret giving up Dean nor did she want to regret cutting short her education. She didn't want her dad to regret letting Olivia go without a fight.

He seemed too broken to argue about the trip to Olivia's to collect his clothes. Suzanne handed him the car keys and opened the front door.

23

The sound of the mobile roused everyone. Olivia felt the physical touch of the knife blade on her skin at the same moment the ringtone pierced and broke her dream. Despite still being vertical, her head had been nodding in the way it did when she was in the passenger seat on long car journeys. She blinked her eyes. It was bright outside but the dining room lights were still on. Wayne was invisible behind her. Tina looked startled. The arm around her neck had been relaxed and resting on her shoulder while they both dozed standing up. Now it was suddenly tight again.

The mobile phone shouted again.

"It's my mobile, in the kitchen. I should answer it," Olivia said.

"No! Leave it." Tina's voice was croaky. "They'll think you're still in bed."

Help was so near and yet so far. Just a swipe would bring the real world in and extinguish this unreality. With each unanswered ring it felt like her sanity was slipping away again. The phone went silent. Thirty seconds later it beeped. The caller had sent a text message.

"Should we have breakfast? Coffee at least? That sponge

pudding and custard was a long time ago." The brightness in her voice was false. She was working on the premise that making a friend of your captor lessened the probability of them killing you – isn't that what they said on TV survival programs? And maybe it would also give her access to the kitchen and her phone.

"That's a good idea." Wayne's voice, from behind Olivia's head, was hopeful. "My stomach thinks my throat's been cut."

"No."

The landline in the hallway started ringing. Tina shook her head before Olivia had the chance to frame any words. After eight rings the answer machine cut in and the speaker was clearly audible.

"Olivia, it's me." Tina's expression showed Olivia that she'd recognised Simon's voice as well. "Pick up, please. It's urgent. All last night, I kept thinking that Tina wouldn't have tried any of this blackmail stuff without real proof. And, if Mum had written down the truth I wanted to see it. I wanted that closure and peace of mind. This is about my parents, my flesh and blood. It's my family history – part of who I am. Even if I couldn't bring the paper away with me and relieve Tina of her power, I wanted to see it with my own eyes. So I went back to the flat at first light this morning. I was going to demand that Tina show me that paper – just so that I knew the truth."

The atmosphere in the dining-room had become supercharged. Olivia fought the urge to call out to the disembodied voice. Simon wouldn't be able to hear and she'd drown his message with her yells. Tina had her head cocked to one side, a frown of concentration etched across her forehead. Wayne was fidgeting behind Olivia's back. Please don't let him need to go to the toilet in the middle of this. Please let me hear the rest of this message.

"I hammered on the door of the flat. It was too early for them to have gone out. No one answered. So, I put my arm back through the broken glass, released the door lock and went in. And, get this, Tina and Wayne never went home last night after leaving your place. Their beds weren't slept in. Weird…" For a second the call broke up. Simon must be in the car on his hands free. "… I remembered I never searched the lounge properly. For some reason I was sure the paper must be in the bedroom. So, I pulled the cushions off the settee. There was a pile of women's magazines. I picked up and shook each one. And guess what came out of the third one?"

Tina gasped. Olivia felt an expanding bubble of panic fill her chest. The proof did exist. It was not a figment of Tina's imagination sitting in a fictitious safety deposit box. The proof was there to send Olivia to prison for a very long time.

"I didn't throw it—" Wayne began excitedly.

"Shush!" Tina and Olivia gave the order in unison.

"You need to read it, Liv. I feel so much better knowing how my mother felt and her gratefulness towards you. I'd like to hang on to this paper as a keepsake to her and her selflessness. But, given the contents, I know that's not wise. I'm on my way to you now. Once you've seen it and know what she felt, I think it will be easier for you to forgive yourself. Then we'll destroy it together and watch Tina and Wayne disappear at speed into the sunset."

A click from the machine confirmed the message had ended.

"I think we'll wait here a bit longer." Tina's voice was still calm but there was an edge of menace. "I disagree with Simon's comment about forgiving yourself, Olivia. You haven't suffered enough yet. And I want my property back from Simon. Then we've got a wedding to book."

"You said it was in a bank vault!" Olivia's sleep-starved brain was struggling to keep up with the pace of events. "And I knew that couldn't be true. Banks don't offer that service anymore."

"We thought the paper was lost so Tina made that up." The vibes from Wayne's body behind her were changing. He'd become bouncy and positive, his voice full of pride and pleasure.

"But I didn't mess up. I didn't throw away the wrong thing. I remember putting the magazines under the cushion but I never saw no paper. But I didn't throw it away!"

Tina ignored her brother's comments. "When we've got that piece of paper from Simon, we'll have that coffee you're offering." Tina's face was happier, pinker, her eyes brighter. She stood up more easily. "Call it a little celebration."

The doorbell rang and was immediately followed by hard rapping with a metal knocker. Nobody moved. Thirty seconds of silence. More doorbell ringing and banging. Olivia looked towards Tina. The other woman looked as though she was trying to work out the best course of action.

"Shout that you're in the bath," she instructed. "Ask him to push it through the letterbox."

"Simon?" No answer from beyond the door – her voice was too quiet, dampened by the fear swamping her body and the arm constricting her throat.

At the nod from Tina, Wayne loosened his grip so that Olivia could project her voice. False courage plus an open windpipe amplified her words like a loudspeaker. "I'm in the bath! Push it through the letterbox!"

"OK!" There was a metallic clatter from down the hallway. Then a voice that sounded close enough to touch, spoke through the narrow slit. "Call me when you've read it."

"Will do!"

The letterbox clattered shut. Everything must seem normal to Simon, there was nothing outside the house to indicate the siege taking place within. Tina waited a few minutes and then went to collect the delivery. She held the single sheet of paper in front of Olivia but at slightly more than arm's length away from her. "We don't want you making a grab for it, do we? It wouldn't do to get this precious piece of paper damaged."

Without her reading glasses, Olivia had to screw up her eyes to make sense of the handwriting. As she digested the words, a lump formed in her throat. It astonished her that Audrey could still be so generous with her gratitude after experiencing the hell of prison for several years. Surely that incarceration must have been far worse than life with her abusive husband? If Audrey was writing truthfully about her emotions, could Olivia finally let herself believe she'd done the right thing by not speaking up about her guilt earlier? Did this letter give her a blessing to get on with the rest of her life?

"So, shall we get that wedding date fixed and get a pre-nup in place?" Tina's voice echoed the 'I told you so expression' on her face. "If you divorce Wayne after I'm gone, I want to make sure he's financially well provided for."

The letter might have lessened the guilt but there was still going to be no happy ever after for Olivia. "I don't think that's how pre-nups work—"

"What you think doesn't matter. You'll do what I say unless you want to be driven to suicide in prison, like Audrey."

The doorbell rang again. Tina put a finger to her lips. With the other hand she anchored Audrey's piece of writing to the dining table with the cream jug. The knife blade was touching Olivia's throat again, she didn't dare call for help. The metal knocker sounded. The three of them were statues, only their eyeballs moved. There was the sound of a key in the lock. Olivia's heart soared and then plummeted. Mark had to be kept out of this mess. She'd wrecked his life enough already. If he came in now he'd find out the terrible truth about her past.

"Go away!" Olivia didn't wait for permission from Tina before she shouted. She was past caring about herself – she just wanted to protect the ones she loved.

***

The sharp command took Suzanne by surprise, Olivia had never spoken so harshly before. But she was already in the hall and Dad needed those clothes. "I'm sorry, I thought you were out when no one answered the door. I won't be more than two minutes."

There was no reply. Suzanne pushed the front door shut behind her and slipped the key back into the pocket of her jeans. Out of habit she sat on the bottom step and pulled off her trainers. She expected Olivia to appear and welcome her from the kitchen or at the top of the stairs.

"Dad sent me to get some of his stuff," Suzanne called. "He's run out of clean clothes."

Still no sound from anywhere. She could go upstairs and grab some T-shirts and underwear and disappear again without disturbing Olivia but she'd forgotten to bring a bag to put the stuff in. There was always a pile of old carrier bags in the kitchen. Olivia wouldn't mind if Suzanne took a couple. She walked down the hall. As she moved towards it, the dining room door swung almost closed. It paused, slightly ajar, and then closed snugly in the frame. Suzanne froze. The only way that could happen was if someone had gently pushed it shut from inside the dining room. If Olivia was in there, why hadn't she come out to say hello? It was definitely Olivia's voice that had called out as she opened the front door.

"Are you in there?" She spoke to the wooden interior door. The absence of a reply was too loud.

Suzanne glanced at the open kitchen door. The easiest thing would be to get a carrier, grab Dad's stuff and leave. It was pointless upsetting Olivia by trying to talk to her, she obviously wasn't in the mood for visitors. Suzanne extricated two supermarket plastic bags from the pile in the cupboard next to the cooker. The kitchen was messier than Olivia usually left it. From the detritus it looked like she'd had visitors the previous evening and had only got round to half-loading the dishwasher. There were dishes with the remnants of custard still on the worktop and the door of the dishwasher was open showing dirty plates and three wine glasses. Olivia didn't leave tasks half-completed like this. Something wasn't right in this house. It reminded Suzanne of the Marie Celeste. She'd stayed over several times and Olivia had never left it until the morning to clear away. Even on the night of the engagement party she'd resisted Dad's pleas to go to bed and leave the mess until the following day.

"Are you OK, Olivia?" Suzanne stood right next to the dining room door and raised her voice. "Do you want to talk?"

"No." Olivia's voice sounded mangled.

Did it mean, no, she wasn't OK or no, she didn't want to talk?

"Shall I come in?" Suzanne placed her hand on the door handle. "You don't sound well."

"No!" It was still mangled but louder and there was fear there too.

24

Something was so not right in this house. And the thing that was not right was behind this door into the dining room. Suzanne's heart could no longer keep a steady beat. The thoughts in her head were dark. The humiliation in the church could have disturbed Olivia's mental state and affected her judgement. What if… what if… Suzanne hardly dared to think: what if Olivia had decided to kill herself? What if she'd slit her wrists, taken a million pills or done something else? What if she was sitting in the dining room waiting for it to take affect? What if she was hanging in there, dangling from a makeshift noose on a homemade gallows, waiting for her neck to break?

Suzanne's knees went weak. She took a deep breath and opened the door to the dining room.

"Run away, Suzanne!" The second syllable of Suzanne was squashed into inaudibility.

A big man had Olivia in a stranglehold. It was the man from the church, the same one Olivia had been with on the estate. Suzanne wanted to turn and flee as instructed but she was mesmerised by the scene in front of her. In his other hand the man had a knife. There was blood on Olivia's throat and on the collar of her blouse.

"Go!" Olivia grunted again, her eyes wide and staring intently at Suzanne, as though trying to amplify the message.

Suzanne turned to leave as the dining room door clicked shut. A thin woman was leaning on it. In her shock at seeing Olivia, Suzanne hadn't noticed a third person in the room.

"She gave you enough warning and you didn't go. Now you don't have a choice." The voice was evil, as though the woman was copying a TV actress in a horror film or something.

This had to be a robbery gone terribly wrong – the kind of thing *Crimewatch* specialised in.

"What's going on? Olivia, tell them where your jewellery is. Give them your cash." Why hadn't Olivia handed everything over and allowed the burglars to escape? No necklace or ring could have so much value, sentimental or financial, that made it worth risking your life. "Give them what they want. Dad…" Suzanne suddenly thought better of it and didn't mention her waiting father. She looked over at the patio doors. The key had been removed from the lock. No point trying to escape that way. She pulled her phone out of the back pocket of her jeans.

"No phone calls!" The thin woman moved towards her awkwardly and knocked the phone to the floor. Then she stamped on it, hard, very hard, with the heel of her court shoe. Splinter lines shot across the glass screen.

"But my dad…"

"Your dad doesn't matter. He's nothing. He's like an annoying bit of chewing gum stuck beneath your shoe. Olivia doesn't want him anymore. She's going to marry Wayne – the wedding will be very soon. Wayne, show Suzanne how much you two love each other."

The evil woman was so compelling that Suzanne daren't look away from her. There was something about her eyes. Then a sudden loud sigh and grunt from Olivia made Suzanne turn round. Wayne had released his arm lock on Olivia's neck. Now, he and she stood hand in hand. The knife was hanging in Wayne's free hand. Wayne was grinning and casting proud glances at Olivia. Olivia stared at the floor.

The doorbell rang again. Everyone's eyes swivelled towards the dining room door and the noise that came from beyond. The knocker rapped, metal on metal. It must be her dad, finally fed up of waiting in the car. She'd tried to persuade him to come in with her and be civilised to Olivia but he'd refused point blank. Impatience must be getting the better of him.

The group in the dining room was silent, all looking to Tina for direction. Suzanne didn't dare say who was at the door.

Tina allowed a few minutes to pass after the final bang on the door, then she picked up where she'd left off. "Olivia, give your fiancé the respect and love he deserves."

Olivia did nothing.

"Look at him!"

Olivia raised her head towards Wayne who was a few inches taller. She didn't meet Suzanne's eyes and her face was devoid of expression. She looked like a broken woman. Wayne bent and kissed her on the lips. Olivia's head recoiled but couldn't tip far enough back to escape his searching mouth. The kiss was much more than a polite social peck and Suzanne turned away from Olivia's humiliation.

"See what I mean?" Tina said. "They're two lovebirds. You can still be a bridesmaid. It would be a shame to waste that lovely dress."

This woman was a psycho and should be locked away. The shock and fear that had hit Suzanne as she entered the dining room was rapidly being replaced by sparks of anger. Something must have happened to make Olivia so submissive but Suzanne wasn't going to stand for it. "Why are you doing this?" she demanded of Tina.

Tina glanced at Olivia before answering. Then she smiled. "It's complicated. A long story, you might say. In a nutshell, I'm dying of cancer. Wayne needs emotional and financial security after I'm gone. With a little bit of persuasion from me, Olivia has agreed to provide that, in the form of marriage." With difficulty Tina manoeuvred the dining chair she'd been sitting on and used it to block the door shut. She sat down again and folded her arms.

Suzanne looked from the thin, hard face of Tina to Olivia's soft but desolate expression. Taking in Tina's grey skin, her slow, awkward way of moving and the occasional grimace of discomfort, she surmised the older woman was telling the truth, she was seriously ill. But why would Olivia agree to this marriage? Suzanne looked at her expecting some sort of explanation but Olivia simply shook her head sadly. There were shadows under her eyes and tired makeup that must have been there since last night. Her face was a mask of shame and sadness.

Wayne raised his knife again and the tension in the room increased. Suzanne's brain went into overdrive. She didn't understand the situation. There was too much left unsaid. All she knew for sure was that this man and woman had destroyed the lives of at least three people, Olivia, Dad and herself. In no way could that be right. Fury flowed through her like hot lava. It poured into her mind, leaving no room for rational thought.

Suzanne threw herself towards Wayne, targeting the arm that held the knife. "Get away from her!" she yelled and, keeping her eyes on the blade, she tried to hold his arm still and prise open his fingers so that he dropped the weapon.

"No, Suzanne! Leave it." Olivia stumbled away, free. Wayne needed two hands to fend off Suzanne.

Suzanne kicked at his shins but without shoes her feet were powerless and she stubbed her toes. But she refused to give in. She sank her teeth into the flesh around the base of his thumb. There was a slight taste of salt and then a metallic undertone. She realised she'd drawn blood and immediately released her jaw. Nausea mixed with the anger in her stomach.

"Bitch!" Wayne held the top of Suzanne's right arm with the squeezing pain of a vice. His other hand held the knife centimetres from her chest.

Fear quashed all other emotion. She was going to die. Her life did not flash before her eyes like it should. Maybe it had been too short or not well lived. All she saw was the blade. He had body odour and bad breath. That kiss Olivia received must have been revolting. His face had turned puce. Any minute now she'd feel the blade enter her chest. How long before she bled to death? Would her heart stop? Or perhaps her lungs would deflate and she'd gasp for breath like a fish out of water. All these thoughts fitted between a single tick of the clock.

Then her legs went from under her. A great force was pushing her away from him. He struggled to keep his grip on her and failed. It was a hard landing and her head thumped against the leg of a chair. There were bright stars in the blackness of her mind and a weight landed on top of her, knocking the remaining wind from her lungs. It was Olivia. Somehow she'd rugby tackled Suzanne to the floor and placed herself closest to the knife.

"Grab the paper from the table!" The words were stuffed into her ear as Olivia rolled away from Suzanne and closer to the knife.

Suzanne dizzily raised herself to a kneeling position. The tablecloth shielding her from Tina. She raised her head and scanned the table top. Grabbed the paper and, in doing so, sent the cream jug tumbling in Tina's direction.

"Get the girl!" Hysteria entered the thin woman's voice for the first time.

Olivia was back, almost on top of her again. Suzanne pushed the balled up paper at her. She saw Olivia stuff it in her pocket as Wayne stood over both of them with the knife.

"Olivia's worth nothing dead." Tina was regaining control. "Stab the girl – give her a warning to keep her mouth shut."

Wayne dragged Olivia to her feet and away from Suzanne. A thunderous bang on the patio window turned all their heads. With his concentration diverted, Wayne tripped. It was like watching a slow-motion replay. The big, clumsy man falling with the knife in his hand. Simultaneously, there was a movement in Suzanne's peripheral vision. Olivia diving towards her from a shorter distance, landing on Suzanne and then a scream. Everything blotted from Suzanne's view and she coughed on a mouthful of hair. Female swearing. More thudding on double-glazed glass.

"Is she dead?" Wayne's voice, muffled by a choke of misery.

Panic growing in her chest. Heaving the deadweight of Olivia off. Sitting up and seeing the blood! She looked down at the body prone on the floor, the wet, scarlet puddle on the front of Olivia's blouse slowly expanding. Suzanne held up her own hands and stared at the smeared crimson swirls – the red symbol of death embedded in the lifelines of her hands. Wayne kneeling, crying, blood on him too. Not even a massacre could have this much blood. Tina stood at the door, unmarked by the crimson stain of blame, urging Wayne to get up and leave. The crushed mobile. Gambling that they won't hurt her further if she dashes to the landline. First 999 call of her life. Cordless phone at her ear, returning to hold Olivia's hand. Shouting from the front door. Wayne and Tina are gone. Her dad is here. The ambulance is here.

They're not allowed in the ambulance. Dad drives the car. He's asking her questions but it's too soon. She hasn't processed stuff herself yet. She can't answer him. The blood on her clothes is awful. They have to operate. She and dad are left in a waiting room. There's a drinks machine. After a while she fumbles coins in a slot and slops watery hot chocolate over the edge of a plastic cup. Her hands shake too much. It goes cold on the table. Dad with his head in his hands, mumbling regrets about not letting Olivia explain and jumping to conclusions.

Police arrive. She has to focus and explain. A new plastic cup with sweet tea. She manages it without spilling. They want detail. She has to shut her eyes and relive the horror like pressing 'play' on a film. There's a plastic envelope containing a handwritten essay. The police ask if she's seen it before. They don't show her father. Telling them about grabbing the paper from the table and Olivia pushing it in her pocket. She can't be sure it's the same sheet.

A doctor says she's out of theatre. Five minutes to stand and look at her. She's not conscious. It's like on TV with drips and tubes and machines. Beeps. Rhythmic beeps. Then home. A shower. Very long and very hot.

25

Olivia asked for Mark as soon as she could talk coherently. It was the afternoon of the day after her admission and they told her he'd been sitting in the waiting room since 8 am. After all that had happened she couldn't believe he was so eager to see her. The nurse who seemed to be in charge said they could have ten minutes together and then the police wanted to speak to her.

"I have to tell you something," she said. She was propped on pillows and talking with some difficulty. Mark was holding her hand. She managed a squeeze – his touch was something she'd craved over the past week. "The police or Suzanne might have already told you?"

He shook his head. She was glad – this was an explanation that she owed him and he shouldn't hear it from anyone else. It was unfinished business and something she should have told him as soon as they got serious about one another. He would walk away when he knew but that was for the best now, she didn't want to drag him down with her when she was convicted. But at least he would leave knowing the truth and not whatever story he'd made up in his own mind. Or whatever tale the press chose to print when the story got out.

"The nightmares about the murder of Simon's father. I

didn't tell you the whole story." Then she told him everything as plainly and honestly as she could.

Part way through he let go of her hand. He shook his head.

When she'd finished he repeated "How could you?" several times. Then he left. There was no hug, no kiss, no forgiveness, no nothing. She knew it was the end. No one would want dragging into the gutter with her. But at least she'd told him herself.

Talking to the police was easier – their opinion of her didn't matter as much.

***

Olivia could hear Suzanne speaking to a nurse. She closed her eyes and pretended to be asleep again. Eventually the teenager would get the message and stop turning up at the hospital. She wanted Suzanne untangled from her life with the same clean break Mark had decided on. There'd been no contact from him since she'd told him she was a murderer. On reflection, that was best for Mark and Suzanne. Her own physical wounds would heal but the stigma that had surfaced with Audrey's writing would never leave her. Only a few people had seen Audrey's account of her husband's murder but when it came to trial the whole world would know. There would be finger-pointing, talking and people giving her the cold shoulder. Everyone close to her would suffer. She didn't want them dragged down too. It was best she made the break with them all now.

The hospital had put her in a side room because of the police visits. Gradually, as she improved physically, the officers had been allowed to spend longer at her side asking questions. Sometimes they talked about Tina and Wayne and sometimes they went back three decades. She knew they'd talked to Simon too, as the only other living witness to the historical case. He'd been to see her a couple of times. He was the only one she'd speak to, except the police. Joanne had also been given the back of the head treatment.

Simon had told her how upset Suzanne was when Olivia wouldn't speak but she refused to let his words change her mind.

"She knows you're only pretending to be asleep. She says when you're turned away from her she can see your reflection in the window and your eyes are open."

"I don't want her hurt any more than she has been. When the press get hold of what I did, I don't want anyone else dragged through the mud with me, least of all a teenage girl with her whole life before her."

"You're over-dramatising things. You saved her life, for God's sake. She wants to thank you to your face not the back of your head."

"Now who's over-dramatising? I only did what anyone else would have done, given that it was my fault she was in danger anyway."

"Have it your way but I don't think she's going to give up."

Simon was right. Each day after school Suzanne sat on the hard plastic chair for forty-five minutes and talked about the outside world. She told Olivia about the end-of-term events she was helping to organise in her new role as prefect; a concert by the year sevens and an alternative sports day including three-legged and wheelbarrow races.

"It's like being back in junior school but much harder. I'd forgotten that being a wheelbarrow requires so much upper-body strength."

She also talked about Mark.

"He's been forced back to work. Somebody from HR came out to see him, a nice lady but she said that without a sick note he had to return to work, or get signed off by the doctor. He doesn't like doctors so he went back to work. He said the first day was awkward. The whole office was subdued and there was no banter. It was like someone had died but there was no body.

I told him that going forward things would only be as bad as he made them. So on day two he went prepared to lighten the atmosphere and started a couple of football arguments. After that it was OK. Since then he's been on the up and much more proactive."

Mark was getting on with his life, it was hard but she forced herself to be glad about that. Eventually Suzanne would run out of things to say and go home.

"In you go," said the nurse to Suzanne as usual. "But I don't think she's going to be any more receptive than yesterday."

"She will be." Suzanne's voice sounded confident.

Olivia closed her eyes. She had no wish to hear any more about how Mark's life was on the up. Bully for him and his proactiveness. She wanted to put her hands over her ears but that would've shown she wasn't asleep. Footsteps came around the bed on the vinyl floor.

"I know you're awake. And I'm fed up of the rude way you're treating me. Anyone would think you were the sulky teenager – that should be my role."

Olivia opened her eyes. Suzanne was crouched at bed height staring right at her.

"You might have become self-centred and uncaring," the girl said, "but I haven't. Right now, and in the coming months, you're going to need friends and I'm going to be you're number one friend, along with Joanne."

There were more sounds of shoes on vinyl and Joanne appeared in Olivia's line of sight. Olivia felt nothing but shame. Her best friend knew she was a murderer. The girl she'd hoped would become her stepdaughter knew she was a murderer. They'd both taken pity on her like some do-gooding prison visitors.

"I don't want your pity. I don't want you to stand by me because that's the 'right' thing to do. Go home and let me wallow in my own shame."

Suzanne and Joanne exchanged glances. Olivia turned over and faced the door.

"We'll come back later," said Joanne. "You've got another visitor right now."

Mark appeared in the doorway. Olivia took a sharp breath and forgot to let it out until her lungs complained. She wanted to pull the covers over her head and disappear but more than that she wanted to look at him. Now he was here, in front of her and close enough to touch, she realised how much she'd missed him. She'd told herself she could cope alone, she didn't need anyone but now the thing she wanted most in the world was to be held tightly in his arms. She wanted him to stand by her. But she wouldn't ask him to do that.

Neither of them spoke. He looked tired. She probably looked worse. Suzanne and Joanne left the room muttering something about fetching tea. Olivia pushed herself up into a sitting position. She had trouble arranging the pillows behind her. Mark leaned over to help. His hand brushed the bare skin of her arm. There was a spark. And then he moved and sat down on the hard chair.

"I'm sorry," she said, "for everything. I should have told you the truth much earlier, especially when the nightmares started."

"Yes, you should." His tone gave away his disappointment.

She guessed he'd come to officially terminate their relationship. She should give him back her engagement ring, only she didn't know what had happened to it.

"It was good of you to come. We can both move on now. I hope you find that special someone you deserve."

He was frowning. "Is that what you want?"

"Isn't that what you want? You can't want a murderer."

"Suzanne made me talk to Simon. He's convinced me you killed his father to protect his mother. You didn't mean to kill him, only to stop him hurting her."

The tears started. When she sobbed it hurt her still-healing chest. She tried to regain control.

"And you definitely saved Suzanne's life by risking your own. I saw that with my own eyes. That made me rethink our whole relationship." He passed her a tissue and then another one. "You are not a murderer, you are a lifesaver and I do want you. I want you as soon as possible."

Olivia reached for his hand and squeezed. He bent towards her, she raised her face and they kissed.

"You might have to wait a long time," she said slowly. "The trial judge may decide that I am a murderer and lock me away."

"That's a possibility. But together we'll get the best lawyer we can afford. And we can be married before then – if you still want me?" His last sentence was hesitant and his eyes were questioning.

"What?"

"Will you marry me, Olivia?"

"Yes!"

A cheer erupted from the doorway. Suzanne and Joanne came in carrying two plastic cups of tea each.

Joanne put hers down on the bedside cabinet and pulled four mini packets of custard creams from her handbag. "It's all the vending machine would let me have but it's enough to get the celebration going!"

"You two knew already? It was planned?"

"Absolutely," said Mark, his hand still in hers. "I checked your bail conditions and we have an appointment at the registry office next week to give notice that we want to be married. I've checked with the consultant and there's no reason why you shouldn't be home by then. Within six weeks we can be married."

There were more voices at the nurses' station outside on the main ward.

"She's got three visitors already. Perhaps you could wait until one leaves."

"It's important. I've got some news for her." It was the voice of the policeman who'd taken her statement and asked most of the questions.

The hope that Mark had brought dissolved.

Joanne and Suzanne looked at each other. "We'll disappear again."

The policeman pulled a chair from the opposite side of the room across to the bed. "I wanted you to know as soon as possible," he said. "Tina died this morning. She was in the hospital wing and it was peaceful. The doctors think that Saturday night put too much strain on her."

"I see." What is there to say when an enemy dies? Olivia felt pity for the woman but not sadness. She felt anger that there would be no punishment and, despite what he'd done to her, regret that Wayne would have to cope alone. At least she had Mark.

"Wayne is undergoing psychiatric assessments," the policeman continued. "We don't yet know whether he'll be deemed fit to stand trial."

"I see." It looked like she was going to be the only one to stand in a dock.

***

As Mark had promised, the wedding took place six weeks later in the registry office. He looked incredibly handsome in his morning suit and top hat. When he said, 'I do', Olivia cried. When she said, 'I do', he hugged her like he would never let her go.

Joanne had a sapphire and diamond ring on the fourth finger of her left hand. She and Simon barely left each other's side throughout the ceremony and the lunch that followed. Olivia hugged them both and wished them every happiness together. She had no idea whether or not she'd be free to attend their wedding in six months' time.

Suzanne walked tall in her silver dress and the eyes of an awkward looking youth never left her. After the ceremony she introduced Dean to Mark and Olivia. Mark frowned but shook his hand and said it was a pleasure. Olivia kissed him. Suzanne looked grateful. It was obvious from watching them together that the relationship wouldn't last. But while it did, the couple deserved the courtesy of being treated with respect.

Bail conditions wouldn't stretch to a honeymoon but those few weeks grace before the court case were magical.

ABOUT SALLY JENKINS

"Sally Jenkins knows how to build a story. She takes the mundane, and makes it intriguing. She hooks the reader, and reels him in... her capacity for twisting each tale's ending is nothing short of phenomenal." – Readers' Favorite Book Review Website.

Sally's stories have been successful in a range of competitions and magazines. She has twice won the Friends' of Morley Literature Festival Short Story Competition, was the 2014 Disney Winnie the Pooh Laureate of the Midlands and in 2016 was shortlisted in the Just Write Creative Writing Competition.

Sally's debut novel, Bedsit Three, a psychological thriller, was published in October 2015. It won the Ian Govan Award and was shortlisted for the Silverwood-Kobo-Berforts Open Day Competition.

Sally lives in north Birmingham with her husband and their goldfish, Reg. The wilderness of Sutton Park is close by, a wonderful place for wandering, plotting and creating characters. By day Sally works in IT but after hours she lets her imagination run riot. And when she's not hammering at the keyboard she gets her exercise bell ringing and attending Bodycombat classes.

Follow Sally Jenkins on Twitter: @sallyjenkinsuk
Find out more about Sally and follow her blog at
http://www.sally-jenkins.com

ALSO BY SALLY JENKINS

Bedsit Three

A girl has been buried in a shallow grave. Rain washes away the earth covering her. *Bedsit Three* is a thrilling why-dunnit which twists and turns its way to a shattering finale! No one knows what goes on behind closed doors or in the darkness of our minds. Sometimes the threat is too close to home...

Bedsit Three is a tale of murder, mystery and love. It won the inaugural Wordplay Publishing/Ian Govan Award and was shortlisted for both the Silverwood-Kobo-Berforts Open Day Competition and the Writing Magazine/McCrit Competition.

Michael Barton, Founder and Managing Director of WordPlay Publishing, said of *Bedsit Three*, "It's a book that elicits emotional reaction, drawing the reader into the story and placing him or her in the middle of the action page after page. Be prepared for a sleepless night, because you won't want to put it down until you get to the end."

Available in paperback from Amazon and on all major ebook platforms.